DONE WITH
THE TALKING

DON'T MISS THE NEXT
ROCK SMITH ADVENTURE

"OUT OF CONTROL"

COMING SOON

DONE WITH THE TALKING

NORM COLE

Copyright © 2012 by Norm Cole.

Library of Congress Control Number: 2012909164
ISBN: Hardcover 978-1-4771-1569-5
Softcover 978-1-4771-1568-8
Ebook 978-1-4771-1570-1

All rights reserved. No part of this book may be reproduced or transmitted in any form or by any means, electronic or mechanical, including photocopying, recording, or by any information storage and retrieval system, without permission in writing from the copyright owner.

This is a work of fiction. Names, characters, places and incidents either are the product of the author's imagination or are used fictitiously, and any resemblance to any actual persons, living or dead, events, or locales is entirely coincidental.

This book was printed in the United States of America.

To order additional copies of this book, contact:
Xlibris Corporation
1-888-795-4274
www.Xlibris.com
Orders@Xlibris.com
116918

This book is dedicated to my grandchildren: Zack, Elizabeth, Mike, Dan, Sarah, Alexa, Ahnah, Aleah, Nick and Bill for the joy they gave me when telling them stories about my life.

To authors like Louis L'Amour, Vince Flynn, John Grisham, Brad Thor, and David Baldacci—they know how to tell a story. They have provided me with the incentive to write this novel about our messed up America.

INTRODUCTION

This book makes no effort to further identify the issues that are destroying the United States, but it proposes a hypothetical strategy to remove the cancerous problems.

When a doctor identifies a cancerous growth in a human, he does not continue to identify the growth again and again. He goes directly to the growth and removes the tissue. It could be said that this book takes a medical approach in discussing how to bring back the old values that were laid out by the U.S. Constitution.

In every household and from every media source

there is constant identification of huge problems. Millions of young college graduates cannot find work, millions of homes are in bankruptcy, no money is available to entrepreneurs for building businesses, no permits are given to mine minerals or drill for oil, there are millions of Americans unemployed – the list goes on. There remains a constant discussion of the existing problems, but never a solution to solving them.

This book is about young Special Forces men who spent years in Afghanistan and Pakistan under brutal, dangerous conditions. These men were initially committed to fixing the problems brought on by the Muslims who want to kill us.

These men had high moral values and they wanted to defend the U.S. and its constitution. But upon returning to the U.S., they found that greedy politicians, corporate CEOs and government regulations had created a very different America. These American service men had believed in the good life with a home, a job and a future, only to find that their homes were gone and not any jobs could be found.

During their stay in Pakistan, they found a large

sum of U.S. money that had been scheduled to pay drug farmers for heroin. This heroin would go back to America and be sold on the streets.

They kept the money to fund The Plan to fix America.

There was no violence used in this job to repair America.

These young men decided to cut out the cancer and stop the demise of America.

1

The town of Bruce Crossing lies along the border of northern Michigan on the bottom end of the Upper Peninsula. The town was once a lively community serving the copper mining towns to its north. During the Civil War, President Lincoln had a road built from the northern end of the peninsula to the south, connecting the copper country to U.S. markets. Now timber harvesting keeps people alive, but barely.

From the stoplight in town one can see a lot about yesterday. The feed mill near the corner is almost falling down, the small shop next door is boarded up and the roof has sunk in. Three bars fill another corner, one of them named Alaska. The motel had a recent coat of paint, but the food there was poor and now it's boarded up. The auto dealer to the north of town, at one time a large business, is now an equipment junkyard. The airplane hangars across the highway fly the windsock from a leaning pole along the grass runway.

Caving-in homes with broken windows fill the town. For Sale signs cover the ditches in front of them. Memories are everywhere, but few people. The schools have been closed for years. The fire house remains open with its one 1973 fire engine that's all painted up. That is the fire service for the town.

This was the hometown of Norm Rudy. It was here that he had lived and learned about life. His youth was filled with snowmobiling and chasing down the logging roads on his ATV. His parents had home schooled him and his two brothers. The small Baptist Church was his center of activity. His beliefs in Christian moral values and his God were strong and his attitude about life was positive. Everyone knew him as the Rudy kid, a great worker, a boy with respect for adults. At age seventeen he completed his GED tests for high school graduation and asked his parents to sign for him to join the Marines.

That was five years ago and he was now back home to sort it all out. This was the week his service buddies were to show up in Bruce Crossing. It was Thursday, the 17th of July, and still no one had shown up. There had been no contact between them for six months.

Norm was sitting on a hillside, staring across the cut-over property that his family owned. On the bottom of the gully flowed Moose Creek, cutting its way north to the big river. It had been a long dry summer and the wind blew the tall grass that had already turned brown. Two partridge glided into view and sat in the small grassy areas made by a spring in the hillside. He placed his .17 rifle in the cradle on the front deck of the 800 Can Am 4x4 and focused his scope on one of the birds eighty yards away. The bird showed up like an eagle under the 30 power scope.

Taking the slack out of the trigger, there was a pop from the .17 and the bird tipped over, made a few kicks, and was still. The remaining bird continued to eat the clover, and within a minute Norm started up the ATV, picked up the two birds, and headed back to the cabin. His parents had moved to the city to find work, leaving the old homestead empty.

Norm Rudy was wide and thick in the shoulders, a brooding and cynical young man who trusted no one. His tanned face was one of hard bone, with piercing green eyes. Standing six foot four inches in his socks, he made a statement to those around him. He was now a lonely man. His days of playing his guitar and singing in the small church choir were long behind him. He lived from day to day in his cabin, watching the sunsets.

The times when he hiked the forest of poplar and red pine and lay on the soft moss dreaming about tomorrow were now dim memories. Norm was a man who looked upon life with a dispassionate wry realism. He had seen too much death to believe that life was all that important. He had put in three tours in the Middle East and knew that man lives a brief hour and then went his way and was scarcely missed.

During the last six months of active duty in 2010, he had been assigned to work on a freight plane as a Security Marine; his marine training in Special Forces fit in well with the assignment. He had spent two and a half years on missions in Pakistan and had seen some nasty stuff. His last assignment was good duty, hauling freight across the U.S. from base to base. In January of 2010, his unit was moved to Ellsworth Air Base in South Dakota and from there he started hauling freight to and from the Middle East.

He had returned to his home in Bruce Crossing six months ago at age twenty-two. The world no longer seemed safe or secure. He didn't watch T.V. or read the news; too much tax money was being given away, the economy was bad, unemployment was over eighteen percent in the U.P., and the war was getting bad reviews in Pakistan.

Cleaning up the birds behind the cabin, Norm heard a car door slam out front. After washing off his hands, he walked around the building and looked down the driveway at a yellow Hummer. Frank Mullin had just gotten out of the truck and was looking across the small apple orchard south of the house.

Norm spoke first. "Nice wheels."

Frank turned around and gave Norm a big grin. "Nice place."

They shook hands, Norm picked up Frank's

bag, and they headed into the cabin. The cabin was decent, but nothing too special. It was off the path, quiet and homey. Frank handed Norm a cigar and then they returned to the bird cleaning at the rear of the house.

Frank Mullin had grown up in Rockford, Illinois, in the old part of town. His dad worked in a tool factory, and split his time between it and the bars around town. His mother finally moved out of the house with Frank and his brother – he had very little to do with his dad after the sixth grade.

He was tall and good looking like John Kennedy, with the same brown hair and warm smile. Frank was a fantastic fisherman and hunter as a kid, but the most important thing in Frank's life was sports. He was a natural in all sports in high school. His life was pretty good and he looked forward to going to college, but had no money, so he joined the Marines a few weeks after high school graduation. He figured that the GI Bill would give him a shot at college.

Whatever gentleness lay within him was now hidden behind his dark brooding eyes. His attitude toward strangers showed no visible softness and left no illusions. Frank's life changed when he enlisted in the Marines Special Forces at age eighteen just out of high school. He served two tours in Pakistan with his boots on the ground with a Special Forces detail. He knew lots about killing and believed in the war. His last eight months were served on flight status as a security guard on freight planes stationed out of Ellsworth Air Base.

The land he returned to was not like the one he had left, with its bad economy, a public that didn't like the war, a government that was giving away the tax money like crazy and a White House crew that was trying to make a communist country of the USA. He had contempt for government people and contempt for those around him in authority. He had lost his way. Sports were no longer of interest.

He had been discharged from the Marines just over six months ago and was not interested in college. He had been selling cars for a dealer in Rockford and made enough to eat. He had a room rented in a cheap apartment and just did nothing. Life was different now. Frank and Norm had agreed to meet in Bruce Crossing in mid July of 2011 to make some decisions about the future.

Norm and Frank hung out at the house for a

couple days waiting for Rock Smith. He didn't show. But they knew Rock would come if he were not dead or in jail, so they hung in there, day after day. They had taken a couple 4x4 ATVs out of the shed and were running in the mud on the logging trails near Mass City.

It was pouring rain and the wind was blowing as they wallowed in the muddy trails on their way back to the house. Today was the 26th of July and they were beginning to get worried, but as they came up the hill out of Moose Creek they saw an old blue GMC pickup sitting in the drive. It was Rocky. He was standing out on the deck as they drove up. He waved and came out to meet them in the rain.

Rock Smith was a former Air Force Captain and was responsible for dispatch of all freight both on and off his plane – the same plane that Frank Mullin and Norm Rudy had been assigned to out of Ellsworth Air Force Base in South Dakota.

Rock came from a family of eight kids. His father was a wolf trapper in Montana, and his mother cooked and took care of the kids on their small ranch. The Bible was the only reading material in the home and there had been several of them. Rock finished his school years in a country school and was given a baseball scholarship to college.

He was bright, not so good looking, but had a great smile and blond hair. He looked happy all the time and in his yearbook he was voted the most likely to succeed. He loved flying and spent hundreds of hours flying floats in the Canadian wilderness during his college years. Rock was at peace in the mountains of Montana and held that place as home.

Now his face showed deep lines. His head was almost bald. He wouldn't look at people when speaking to them, and a stranger might not be able to guess his attitude. His deep blue eyes showed fear and ruthlessness. The ranch he grew up on no longer was of interest; the girl he had left behind was long gone.

About seven months ago, he got out of the service with the rank of Captain and a soured view of the world, having done too much hauling of dead and wounded GIs from the Middle East. Living in a small cabin he had built in Montana after returning from Pakistan, he did some flying from time to time to make a living. He was disgusted with the media and with the government and felt that life was a fake.

The reason he was two weeks late for the meeting was that he had been in a treatment center for booze the past month.

Life sucked.

2

six months earlier

The clouds were thick enough to walk on. It had been that way for the past nine hours. For a while Norm had been able to see the ocean below when the clouds opened and closed for a brief moment, but not anymore – it was solid clouds. They were flying at twenty-eight thousand feet and were still almost six hours away from Pakistan. It would be dark when they arrived. They always went into the area during the night due to shelling from the ragheads. This would be his eleventh trip to the war zone, and every time the anxiety was the same, never knowing what to expect, always making final preparations should he not return to Ellsworth AFB.

The sound of the turbo props humming and radio transmissions going back and forth created a numbing effect. The plane was carrying fifteen tons of ammo and parts for ground equipment. The return trips always included broken gear, troops, and stuff. Although the same procedures took place each time, it never became routine, but was always nerve-racking work.

Captain Smith was going through the plane, and he stopped by Norm. "How are you doing, Sarg? Staying awake?"

"Oh, ya can't go to sleep in this racket," responded Norm.

"Well, try and get some shut-eye. It's going to be a long night, and there's lots of stuff to do tomorrow," replied Captain Smith.

Norm nodded his head and returned to his Louie L'Amour saga. Mullin was asleep in his bunk above his head. The freight bay in the plane was huge. The sides of the plane looked like walls of ladders and ratchet straps. Everything was bound down to keep the weight from shifting in rough wind conditions. The bunks were close to twenty feet off the plane floor, and Frank and Norm were on top of all the freight. It was a good idea to have all the stuff as bullet protection, but it involved the use of ladders to get down to the galley and to the johns. The night was long and the closer they got to Pakistan, the more the anxiety increased.

At 02:30 hours the buzzer went off, alerting the crew that they were only thirty minutes out and they needed to prepare for landing. The minutes passed and the engines backed off and the first flaps were put on. The plane started its long descent. Another ten minutes and another flap correction was made as the plane slowed down. Still nothing could be seen outside the plane. They anticipated the next fifteen minutes of zigzagging and sharp declines as the plane maneuvered into airspace for final approach and a high-speed landing. Then they were down. Another perfect landing had been made by Captain Smith.

Mullin, Rudy, Captain Smith and co-pilot Frank Zanon were picked up and driven off to the barracks for a few hours of rest. When the bell rang at 06:00 hours for chow, the dreams stopped and it was reality time again.

The short walk to the chow hall was filled with blowing sand and the sky appeared overcast. It was just another day in sand land. The oatmeal and toast were good, but not home cooking. The hall was filled with GIs, everyone was in a hurry, and the loud speaker was barking out orders to report for duty someplace. They wolfed down the food and turned in their metal plates.

Captain Rock Smith was out by the 6x6 trucks, looking them over as Mullin and Rudy walked over and said, "Good morning, Captain."

Captain Smith looked over at them. "We have a long day ahead of us, guys. We need to move all the records out of a captured building over in Placares and that's forty-five miles away. Four trucks are going over and four weapon carriers to escort us."

The road had been swept during the night for road IEDs, but that was not a sure thing, so the front weapon carrier also had a minesweeper on the front. It was slow going. The GPS systems in the trucks worked well, keeping the trucks on the road in the blinding sand conditions. Between the wind gusts, they caught glimpses of the miles of poppy fields that surrounded the winding road.

At around 14:30 hours, they arrived at the building and parked at the loading docks in the rear. Each of the 6x6 trucks carried a small forklift in the back and these were soon unloaded on the ramp. Captain Smith told everyone to hold off entering the building until he reported back to them. After a sweep around the building with a couple marines, they returned and gave direction to the waiting troops.

There was a large room, almost as big as a gym, filled with file cabinets, desks, and stacks of boxes. Captain Smith said, "Don't take any of the desks, cabinets, or equipment – only records. Put all the boxes into the trucks."

It was getting dark as the truck loads were tied down. All four trucks were filled with boxes and the forklifts hung off the tailgates. The weapon carriers were spread out among the trucks. Overhead the *woff-woff-woff* of two copters running about six hundred feet on each side of the caravan could be heard. The last rays of sunlight had slipped away in the sand clouds and darkness while the troops settled in for the ride back to base. Off in the distance the flare and spark of small firearms broke the night.

Arriving at the base the trucks docked along the

runway and the guys hit the Airmen's Club for a couple beers and then finally off to bed. The flight home was a three-day jaunt, and they hoped to get to Germany by mid-day tomorrow.

The plane had been loaded during the night and was ready for departure by early morning. The C-5 Galaxy's one hundred and twenty foot long storage bay was filled with two tanks, three Hummers, and thousands of boxes of records and HP copy boxes. Rudy had climbed up to his bunk thirteen feet on top of the load during the night and lay down, as the barracks were too noisy to get any sleep. The last of his Louie L'Amour book had ended a half hour ago, and he still couldn't sleep in the noisy airport.

Rudy reached over and slid the cover off one of the boxes, looking for something to read. The box was filled with sealed reams of typing paper. He tried a couple other boxes with the same results. He lay back on his bunk and stared at the ceiling of the plane.

Finally he decided to use his time to write a letter to his folks, and since there were thousands of sheets of paper within his reach, he would help himself. Sitting back up and sliding to the end of the bed, he reached over and removed a box cover, taking out one of the reams of paper. Still half asleep he tore open the ream and stopped cold.

The opened ream of paper revealed sheets of new crisp U.S. one hundred dollar bills! Fresh direct from the U.S. Mint, with seven bills on a page. He removed the wrapper and looked to see if the entire ream was money. It was!

He placed the money back in the box and set it on the bed. Within an hour he had discovered ninety-three copy paper boxes of money, all filled with U.S. one hundred dollar bills. He counted up the data – five hundred sheets to a ream, seven hundred dollars to a sheet, ten reams to a box and ninety-three boxes. Roughly three hundred million in U.S. money!

He had often heard that politicians were sending money over to Pakistan to buy dope from the farmers. The dope was then sent back to the U.S. for sale in America. These politicians had become multi-millionaires since the war started. It was too bad that the building was captured before this money could be paid out to the farmers for dope. Too bad for them, but not too bad for himself, he thought.

A short time later, both Norm and Frank were

speechless sitting up on the load of freight and looking at the boxes of money. Finally Frank said, "There is no way this money is going back to the states and given to some political hack. We need to figure a way to get it someplace for ourselves."

The war-torn minds filled with hopelessness and frustration over life's torment did not allow for any thinking about morality or justice, about doing what was right. What was right in their minds was that the money was theirs… finders, keepers. If it were turned back to the government, it would be sent right back here again. Norm suggested they go find Captain Smith and get his opinion, and that's what they did.

Rock Smith had the same aspirations as Frank and Norm, but how to handle the money was the issue. They were taking the money home, not sure about the details, but sure about keeping it. It was getting near daybreak before a plan was made.

The flight was filled with wind, rain and rough riding as Smith pushed the C-5 Galaxy freighter into the wind toward home. Hours had passed and the drone of the turbo fan engines remained the only sound. Neither Mullin nor Rudy had a clear plan on what to do with the money, but a few questions were first on their minds: how to get the boxes off the base at Ellsworth, where to store them, was the money traceable, what would they do with three hundred million, and the need to remove the ninety-three boxes off the freight manifest.

These were the issues they were talking about when Captain Smith climbed up into the storage area. Rock had a few questions of his own, but mostly they were the same concerns.

Frank asked, "What do you think about redoing the manifest, Captain?"

"I still have the unfinished manifest in my flight bag. I will complete that later. We need to make sure the HP boxes are removed separately from the other cargo when we unload. Frank, I want you to pull a truck in close to the plane immediately and place only the ninety-three boxes on that truck. Then move it out of the way so the remaining freight can be unloaded. We will decide the next step for our boxes afterwards," Rock Smith answered. The discussion continued for another thirty minutes, until Captain Smith returned to the cockpit.

The ten thousand foot runway was quickly eaten

up by the C-5 Galaxy as it made its landing at Ellsworth. The plane was parked at the freight depot area and trucks begin pulling up to the plane for unloading. The area was lit up and traffic handlers were moving about, keeping trucks and personnel in order.

The first truck loaded was with the boxes on the top of the load – the ninety-three boxes of money. When they had been loaded, Frank pulled the truck off to the side and came back to assist with the remainder of the unloading.

The Air Force train that runs along the north side of Ellsworth Air Base was parked at the parameter of the depot loading area. The freight was scheduled to be placed into several railcars and then moved to warehouses around the base. There was also some equipment to be loaded and moved to repair shops in Rapid City, twelve miles away. These shops were leased out to the U.S. Air Force for special purposes.

Captain Smith asked Frank and Norm to move the load of money into the last railcar on the train. So Frank drove the 6x6 over to the loading dock and he and Rudy started quickly moving the boxes into the last car. Frank returned to the depot loading area with the truck and Rudy remained with the train car and the money. The need to monitor the railcar and make sure it left the base was of immediate concern. The flight crew was not scheduled to fly for another week. This time would be used to deal with the money

Boxcar 434 was scheduled to move to Rapid City along with the other boxcars. Taking turns monitoring the railcar for the next two days, they finally received the shipping orders for the trip to town. The train was to leave for Rapid City at 19:00 hours the next evening.

They decided that during the trip across the prairie to Rapid City, the boxcar would be disconnected and car 434 would come to a stop. They would then board the boxcar and load the boxes into Rudy's one-ton pickup truck that had a topper on it.

Lt. Zanon, Rock's co-pilot, had remained in the BOQ for the last couple days and now had come into the officer's mess hall at supper, where no enlisted men were allowed, and sat down with Captain Smith.

"What are you going to do for the next few days, Smith?" he asked.

Rock answered, "I was just thinking about lying around and doing some reading."

"Do you want to do some target practice on the range or something?"

"I don't think so," Rock said.

Zanon remained quiet.

It was 18:30 hours, and the train was moving around at the depot getting ready to haul freight. Frank Mullin moved along the boxcars waiting for a chance to get up into car 434. They had agreed to drop off 434 out on the prairie where a gravel road crossed the rails. They had gone out and checked the spot the day before.

The train moved along the warehouse area, stopping at a half dozen buildings before getting lined up for the trip to town. As the train was about to move out for the trip to town, Frank stepped between the cars and disconnected the airline, leaving only the large roll-over lock holding the cars together. It took only a few seconds. The late fall air was getting crisp as the sun went behind the horizon and the rail cars disappeared into the night.

Rock Smith had stayed clear of the depot until it was time to move off base. As he sat in his room there was a knock at the door. Rock opened the door to find Lt. Zanon. He asked, "Going to chow?"

A slight irritation came over Smith, and he could not help wondering why all the questions from this guy. But, after all, he was Rock's copilot and they did work together. Still, there was something else about the continued contacts he did not like.

"No, I am right in the middle of a good book. I think I will skip chow. See you." He closed the door and stood there, wondering if the Lieutenant had seen the manifest before he deleted the boxes.

After fifteen minutes, Rock walked from the BOQ and got into his GMC. He backed out and headed for the main gate, catching a glimpse of someone walking out from behind a garbage bin as he drove away. He was pressed for time, but could not get his nerves settled about his inquisitive copilot, so rather than going directly to the main gate, he decided to go by the drug store on the base and see if anyone was following him.

After a couple minutes sitting near the rear of the

store, he saw Zanon's blue van drive into the parking lot. Rock sat low in the GMC seat to prevent anyone from seeing him, and waited. Zanon got out of the van and headed into the drug store. Rock quickly moved on around the store and out of sight. He did not see anyone following as he moved through the main gate, but he waited on a side road a few minutes in the dark to make sure. Nothing showed.

As he neared the rendezvous spot, he saw Norm's parked pickup in his headlights. Far off across the prairies he could see the dim light of the train slowly moving towards them. Rock got out and joined Norm in the pickup, waiting for the train to show. As the engine crossed the road, he could see that the last boxcar was no longer connected to the train, yet it moved slowly along behind, coming to a stop just before the crossing. The train continued on into the night.

Norm backed the pickup next to the sliding door of the boxcar as Rock slid open the door. With two of them in the boxcar and one in the back of the pickup, the ninety-three boxes were soon loaded. Norm jumped into the pickup with Frank and they disappeared back down the road toward town.

After twenty minutes, the pickup and Rock's old GMC arrived at the storage building they had rented to store the pickup. The pickup was driven in and the door locked. The three of them headed back to the base in Rock's GMC.

3

Only two days remained before all of them were scheduled to fly back to Pakistan, nothing was said or done about getting a more permanent location for the money. They all agreed not to talk about the money until they returned from the next flight.

But the day of the flight, the C-5 remained on the tarmac for over an hour and then was called back into the flight line and turned off. Captain Rock Smith made a comment to Frank and Norm that he had no idea why the plane was called back. Everyone went off board and the Military Police truck was waiting for the crew when they arrived. All personnel were asked to load up in the truck. Ten minutes later each of the men were placed in private rooms at the MP depot and asked to sit tight.

Captain Smith waited and wondered while the clock ticked by the minutes. Finally Major Cole, the commander of the MPs, showed up. His first comment was cordial as he asked Rock how things were going and the meeting started out pleasantly.

After five minutes the Major began asking some questions. "Were all the boxes and files removed from the captured building in Placares?"

Rock said, "No, there were some remaining boxes left, but all the trucks were filled to the max. I suppose another truckload could be found throughout the buildings but I made a decision that there was not enough left to risk going back for the last load."

Major Cole asked, "Was everything from the building loaded on the plane and delivered to Ellsworth?"

"Yes, all items were delivered and the manifest was turned in following delivery," Captain Smith answered.

Major Cole said, "All the files and boxes have been examined since delivery, and there was information that some valuable documents were to be part of the gathered materials, but they were not found."

Captain Smith said, "Well, it may be worth another trip back to the building when I return, just to make sure nothing was left of value."

The meeting ended. Each of the men were asked the same questions, and since there were several files left and the trucks were completely filled, all the airmen were returned to the plane.

Four hours later the C-5 crossed out of the U.S. air space and headed towards the Middle East. It was not until late in the night, following the landing in Pakistan, that the three of them had a chance to talk about the interviews by Major Cole. Captain Smith had been ordered to make another trip back to the captured building the next day to pick up the remaining documents.

Another day had started and two trucks with two weapon carriers were headed out across the sand. The first hour was routine and then hell broke loose. Out of the sand dunes appeared about sixty Taliban with track vehicles and lots of hardware. The firing started and never let up as the quad-fifties on the weapon carriers laid out borages of firepower at the track vehicles and the ragheads. Captain Smith called in copter fire power from the base. It arrived and ripped up the sand with thousands of rounds, leaving lots of dead ragheads lying in the sand, but not before several of the U.S. troops had died or were wounded.

Only one truck was able to move and the trip was called off. The wounded were transported by one of the copters back to base and the other flew above the 6x6 on its return trip. Since the mission was consider a major requirement, Captain Smith asked the base to furnish a couple copters to fly his crew back to see just what was left at the captured building. Before the sun went down the building was searched and all boxes and file cabinets were searched, but only a few documents were found and put in the copters. Mission accomplished.

Smith wrote out the details of the mission and filed it with the base commander's office, making a second copy to be given to Major Cole on the return trip. The plane was loaded with several GIs returning from duty and others who were wounded. The nineteen foot wide storage area in the C-5 was maxed out.

Upon returning, Captain Smith and Lieutenant Zanon personally met with Major Cole and discussed the mission, and they gave Cole the report on the details. Nothing further was said about another mission to the building, and it appeared that the issue was resolved, at least for now.

It was decided that no discussion would happen with Rock, Frank and Norm in the next several days and they would just let things settle.

Sergeant Rudy requested a three-day pass to go home to see his family and permission was granted. However, there was the issue of Lt. Zanon who seemed very interested in where each of them were ever since they had returned back to base. Also, was he wondering about Norm's missing pickup? Did this create a suspicion?

Finally it was decided that Norm would take Frank's car and drive off the base. Captain Smith and Frank planned to go to a movie in town as a diversion for Zanon prior to Norm's leaving. Rock was to call Norm if anyone followed him towards Michigan on HY I-90.

Rudy signed out for his three-day pass in the late

afternoon and headed for Michigan, or so it seemed. Meanwhile, arriving at the underpass on I-90, Rock pulled over off the road. He got out, lifted the hood, looked all over, and then crawled under his car and jerked at the muffler and clamps, pretending to check them out.

Ten minutes later he saw Norm go on by and turn onto the freeway heading east. After another ten minutes, Rock called Norm and told him Zanon had not shown up. After driving about twenty miles, Norm pulled off the freeway onto a ramp and sat for another fifteen minutes with his hood up. No one showed up, so he did a U-turn and headed to the storage building in Rapid City to get his truck with the money.

It takes about fifteen hours to drive to Michigan, and Norm drove all night, filling up with gas a couple times and grabbing a bite to eat. His last stop was a nervous one. As he was eating, a state trooper came in and sat down by him for a coffee. Norm was in his uniform, the trooper made a few comments about how things were going, and it seemed a normal conversation, but you never knew.

Arriving in Bruce Crossing, Michigan, around

noon the next day, Norm drove the pickup directly into his shop and closed the door. He went into the cabin and sat down in a soft chair, taking a short nap. He had not seen anyone in town, nor did he think anyone had seen him arrive.

The storage plan called for him to build a false wall at the far end of his shop. He had used up almost a day getting to Michigan and needed a full day to return, so lots had to be done. When coming through the town of Ewen, he had called the lumber yard and asked for lumber and sheet rock to be delivered today. He gave the address and was promised that they would be out to Bruce Crossing by early afternoon. Going out to the shop, he removed all the stuff on the wall and the equipment sitting in the way so he could work.

Around 14:00 hours, the lumber truck arrived and was unloaded inside the shop. He drove his pickup with the money into the rear of the shop. By 19:00 hours he had finished putting up the studs and sheet rock. Boxing in the truck behind the new wall, he then went to the cabin for a nap and a sandwich. He returned to the shop and placed all the items back on the shelves on the new wall and it was hard to see that a new wall had been built. He moved all the equipment, hand tools, and power tools back against the wall and cleaned up everything so it looked normal again.

Now he was without a vehicle to return to Ellsworth Air Base. He called his uncle who lived in Mass City and asked him if he would come down and visit, that he had taken a bus home and had no wheels. His uncle arrived shortly after breakfast, and he asked his uncle if he would take him to the car lot south of Bruce Crossing to find a car. An hour later he came back home with a small '04 car that looked like it was able to make the return trip. After putting on a couple burgers, he and uncle had a beer and his uncle left for Mass City. Norm crashed on the couch and woke up at 15:00 hours. He walked out to the shop and checked his work and everything looked like just a normal shop, with no sign of a new wall.

By mid-afternoon the next day he returned to the storage shed in Rapid City, placed his car in storage, and called Frank to come pick him up. He returned to base around 14:00 hours with a couple hours still left on his three-day pass. Rudy was not scheduled to fly for another four days, so he kicked around the base, swimming in the base pool and spending a few hours at the gym. When asked where his pickup was, he just said that it was getting some engine work done and it should be ready when he got back from his next flight trip.

It was time to return to the Middle East again and Norm was waiting on the flight line for the flight crew to show up. He now had a chance to visit before departure with Captain Smith and Frank Mullin about the Michigan trip.

A week later he brought his new car back to the base and told anyone asking about his old pickup that the repairs would have been more than the value of the truck, so he had bought a different auto.

4

Several months passed and Major Cole had not said anything about further information on the documents from the captured building. Zanon had not mentioned the pickup or commented about the mission or any other mission.

Frank Mullin was scheduled to complete his duty at the end of the month or another six days. Rock Smith had checked out of the service a month earlier, and Norm Rudy was to check out in the next three weeks. They had had no visits together and did not think that anyone suspected they had kept any documents. All appeared normal.

Rock Smith had returned to Montana and was living in an old cabin. He had not seen anything suspicious during this time. They had agreed that nothing was to be done with the money for a period of six months after all of them had left the service, which would be around July 15, 2011.

Now here they all were at the Moose Creek cabin in Bruce Crossing, Michigan. Now it was time to make some decisions about the money. During the past six months, none of them had noticed anyone checking on them at the banks or businesses where they lived. Each of them had asked on occasion if any of their service buddies had called or stopped in looking for them. But nothing had happened. Still, there was no peace over this, as the government has a long arm and never gives up if it thinks there is an issue involved with any part of it.

Sitting out on Silver Mountain on the ATVs, they talked about a plan. They decided to test the market to see if the money was being followed by its serial numbers. A Delaware corporation was set up over the internet. The address used was a P.O. Box in Florence, Wisconsin. Ten grand was flown to Delaware by Rock in his old 206 Cessna and deposited at Woods and Lake Bank in Rose, Delaware, under the name of RFN, Inc.

Rock had a phony ID made with the name of Ron Berry, and he signed the bank deposit and the disclosure on the ten thousand dollars with the name of Ron Berry, President. No social security numbers were used, only the RFN, Inc. corporation number. The plan was to wait thirty days to see if anything happened. It is required by a bank to notify the government if more than ten thousand dollars is deposited by a customer. The first contact the government could make would be the post office in Florence, Wisconsin.

Thirty days had come and gone, and it was time to check the P.O. Box. Norm Rudy stopped in the town of Fence, Wisconsin, located three miles south of Florence, and had a few beers in the evening with the locals. He hired one of them, Dell Tipler, a local fishing guide, to take him fishing the next day.

Since Dell was going to Florence to pick up some stuff in the morning, Norm asked him if he could pick up any mail for him in his P.O. Box at Florence. The name on the box was RFN, Inc., and any mail in it should be picked up and brought to him. After telling Dell that he would see him around 11:00 hours tomorrow, he parked his car off the street and walked to the local motel dive where he signed in under a fake name and went to sleep.

Norm checked out early the next day. He drove his car north of Fence and parked on a side road that allowed him to see the highway. There he waited for Dell to return from Florence. He expected that if a notice had been given to the post office to notify the police if anyone picked up the mail that the police would follow Del back to Fence immediately.

Around 09:45 hours he saw Dell's half-ton go by the side road. He waited there for over an hour, and every car that went by either had a family inside or was a clunker. His nerves were up tight. Finally, he decided to make his return trip back to Fence and meet with Dell to see what mail had been picked up. He drove around town for a while, looking for any car or police car waiting near Dell's house. By 11:30 hours he decided to park his car and walk to Dell's house at the edge of town.

Dell was waiting, and wondered where he had been, but Norm told him he had driven around looking at a couple lakes in the area. Dell gave him the mail, and it was a bank statement showing the balance in the RFN, Inc. account. There were no documents about the ten grand deposit, so maybe the money was not traceable.

Norm told Dell that he had changed his mind about fishing, but gave him some money for waiting and thanked him for getting his mail. He got Dell's phone number and told him he would call him later and set up another fishing trip. He walked back along the street and finally went to his car and drove off down the road to the south of town.

Two days later he used a public phone and called Dell asking him what his schedule was for the following day. Dell told him he was tied up until next week. No comment was made by Dell about anyone contacting him about picking up his mail, so it looked like the money was not being traced, or at least not at this time.

Norm used the public phone to call Rock. The signal had earlier been arranged that if all was well at the P.O. Box, he would ask Rock if he would donate to the Fireman's Security Fund.

Rocky said, "No," and hung up.

Frank drove back home to Rockford, Illinois, and Rock flew back to his cabin in Montana. Norm returned to Bruce Crossing.

The next step was to buy a bank so they could deposit the funds in their own bank. This would prevent disclosure on large deposits. The bank they chose was in a small town in southern Wisconsin by the name of Security Bank of Platteville. The ten thousand dollars in the Delaware bank was deposited in the Platteville bank along with another million they had removed from the truck in the shop at Bruce Crossing. They now had one million in place – only two hundred and ninety-nine million dollars yet to find a home. None of the money had been spent, except in buying the bank. No outsiders had made any contact and no suspicious people had shown up.

5

It was now eight months since they had placed their first deposit in their bank, and all was well.

Rocky Smith had been guiding for elk and had kept busy all fall. As he drove up to his cabin with his hunters, he noticed a car parked by his cabin. He did not think anything about it, until the guy got out of his car and met him and the hunters. It was Zanon, with his hunting clothes on. He was friendly, and Rock told him hello and welcomed him into his cabin. The hunters moved on to their cabin.

After visiting for half an hour, Zanon asked, "Could I get a guided elk trip set up with you?"

Rock was nervous, but told him, "I'm booked up for the next week with these hunters, and I don't like to mix hunters with new guests."

Zanon asked him, "Would you talk with them and see what they say?"

"I'll talk with them at supper time," Rock said.

No further discussion was made about hunting and Rock asked, "Do you want to stay for supper and maybe you can get to know these guys a little before I ask them?"

"Sounds like a great idea," Zanon replied.

During supper, one of the hunters asked Zanon about his plans and he told him, "I am an old service buddy of Rock's and I had hoped I could do some elk hunting with him, but it sounds like he is tied up with you guys."

The leader of the group said, "If it's OK with the rest of you, let's take him out tomorrow. We could use the extra person to help drive for pushing out the elk." They all agreed.

By noon the next day two elk had been shot and the work began, cutting and packing them out to the grassy road. Lots of blood and lots of sweat and little talk filled the afternoon. They still needed one elk and they all returned to stands waiting for the elk to move at dusk.

Rock was in his tree stand and was looking through his scope, checking the dark brush for any movement. He saw something move on the top of the hill and, after focusing his scope, he saw Zanon watching him. This was a dangerous position for Zanon and he likely could have been shot if some less experienced hunter had seen him moving in the brush. Rock climbed down and moved up the slope.

He called out, "Zanon, this is Rock. Do you see me?" Zanon came out in the open and walked towards him down the hill.

He said, "Yes, I see you down there." They both continued their walk toward each other.

When they finally met, Zanon said, "Rock, I need to ask you something. I am still wondering what happened to the records that were missing from the mission to Placares?"

Rock stood there looking at Zanon's model 700 Remington rifle and did not respond for a minute. Finally, he said, "What records are you talking about?"

Zanon said, "You need to come clean with me. I think you found something that day and still have it."

Rock removed his woolen cap, showing his balding head and graying hair. His eyes turned glassy and blank. They were ruthless eyes, and his lips were tight. Years of living with a wolfer dad and years of living alone, years of hauling dead GIs, all were reflected in his face.

Rock said, "Mister, anyone calls me a liar when he's holding a gun better find a place to hide or use it. If you don't drop that gun now you will never see the morning." There was no slack in his movement as he placed his rifle barrel on Zanon's belly.

Zanon dropped the rifle and said, "Well, hold on!

You don't need to be so touchy. I was just asking if you knew anything."

Rocky said, "The issue of missing documents was resolved months ago and I have no time for someone like you suggesting that I am dishonest. Leave that gun right where it lays and walk out of here. If you are still at my cabin when I get there I will leave you crippled! If I ever see you again I will beat you within a half inch of your life. Don't ever treat me like some scum from your Chicago world!"

Zanon quickly moved down the hill and out of sight.

6

The three of them were sitting on the mountain east of Mass City having cigars. The news was bad; the country was in serious trouble. Each week another half-million people were put on food stamps. The Tea Parties had tried to make their mark and some new faces were showing up for the election in the fall, but not nearly enough. Glenn Beck continued to preach about the direction the government was headed – socialism for sure or communism maybe. The attitude of the general public was sour and hopeless. Unemployment was climbing every day.

The three of them faced out over the small town below. There were closed up buildings on every block. The church was boarded up and grass grew long on the entry steps. U.S. Highway 26 went down the middle of town and in the past hour not a single car or truck had passed through. The place looked like a morgue. The one gas station had lights on, but no business. There was quietness on the mountain as each of them sat, sullen, yet determined to find a purpose. They had talked about all the problems off and on but just what to do about it was unclear. They had all this money, but how could it be used to help the country?

At last Rock said, "You know, we need to do something to stop all this corruption in the U.S. The recent election gave us a good bunch of Tea Party congressmen, but too few to make a difference. I think that we need to remove some of these individuals messing this country up."

That idea put some direction into their planning.

Rudy said, "I think we should try and get ourselves set up to fix the problems. We know lots about war; it's what we know best. What do you think?"

It was all quiet again as they finished their cigars

and headed back to Bruce Crossing on their ATV 4x4s.

The return trip lasted an hour. That was long enough for each of them to make a decision to move ahead with a plan: to remove crooked CEOs, EPA administrators, and lousy decision makers in Washington, to locate and put away greedy bankers, and to pick up any foreigners that were messing up the country.

7

Zanon returned to Chicago a couple days after his run-in with Rock Smith, puzzled by the deep anger showed by Rock in the mountains of Montana. He was still not convinced that nothing had been found. The amount of concern expressed by Major Cole over not finding anything important suggested that something of real value had been in that building.

Yet nothing showed up even after the second visit to Pakistan. Maybe, whatever was there had been removed before Smith's trucks arrived and that was the end of it… but maybe not.

Zanon had grown up with a suspicious mind.

His family had a long history of gangs and mafia connections. His grandfather had moved from Italy soon after WWII and settled in the Chicago area. As a child, his parents worked hard to keep him from their work and provided him with a good education and a sheltered life.

Now years of flying, facing extreme danger, and looking at GIs shot up or dead, had caused his years of sheltered living to vanish. He was hard, bad tempered, and drank a lot. He found himself with all levels of men and women that walked the streets, where lots of guns and lots of dope were shared by all.

He was determined to find out if something of value had been retrieved from the building in Pakistan, not sure how he would get the answer, but not satisfied that the answer he had been given by Captain Smith was real.

8

The day was hot for June in the U.P. The trees were leafed out and the grass was green; it all looked so normal. Norm, Rock, and Frank sat on the deck at the cabin talking about the details of the plan. The idea they had to weed out those who were stealing our country blind still remained the centerpiece for the Plan – they had some direction at last. Now for the details.

A few weeks had passed and Mullin was leaning against a tree looking out over Pentoga Swamp, a place where he and his friends had spent time roaming the big swamp, deer hunting and trapping wolves for bounty.

Now the three guys were here to evaluate a location to place the crooks. The old log compound that had been used back in the fifties still remained nestled back off the shoreline on the lake. The U.S. Department of Defense had abandoned the place during the Korean War, yet the buildings were still usable. It had first been used during the Second World War as a prison for three hundred German soldiers.

The equipment to operate the place was worthless, yet the buildings were workable. They spent a half day looking at the well, electrical wiring, floors, roofs, windows, and it looked safe for use. The compound was over fifty miles from Florence, Wisconsin, the nearest town. Long Lake was mostly surrounded by swamp with only five acres of high ground touching the lake. In the mid 50's the small creek that drained the lake into the Brule River was dammed up and the creek was now full of wild rice. In the years it was operating, the prisoners were moved into the camp by way of the creek, but now the only way in was by float plane, copter, or ATV.

Frank said, "What do you think, guys, will this do the job?"

Rock looked over at Frank and said, "It will work."

Done with the Talking

Rock's old Cessna 206 amphibian was pulled up on the grassy shore close to the compound. "It will take some time to fill the place with beds and kitchen stuff, board up the windows, sound proof the generator room, and etc., but let's give it a try," Rock said.

"Let's get on out of here and get to work," said Norm.

They loaded into the plane and Rock set up twenty degree flaps for a short field take off and in a quarter of mile they were off the water and heading back to Bruce Crossing. On the way, they talked over The Plan.

Frank said, "Norm and I are going to make contact with some of the International Special Forces guys that we know and put together a few teams to start picking up our first crooks. It will take a few weeks to get the planning done, but the sooner the better."

Rock commented, "I will give my old flying buddy in Montana a call. He owns a couple of Bell Copter 430s that he uses for logging. The logging business is doing poorly and he could use the work, and we have the money to hire him and both his copters."

Rudy was concerned about keeping the Pentoga Compound secure and said, "We need to operate here only at night and we must not alter the grass or trees to suggest that the buildings are being used." They all agreed.

Rock said, "I will start working on getting the camp ready with some food and beds, a generator for power, etc. Most of the equipment that needs to be brought in will fit in the 206 cargo door, but the heavy stuff will have to come in with a Bell 430."

9

Major Mike Nelson had spent years chasing smugglers and about every other killer type across the world and had walked away from the Marines two years ago. Now, filled with a desire to do something good for America, he responded with enthusiasm when asked by Norm Rudy to help with the Pentoga Plan. He had driven to Bruce Crossing, Michigan, and was working with Norm and Frank on the details of how to gather the worst of the worst and put them in isolation until they would talk.

U.S. Senator Henry was seated in a smoky bar room in Flint, Michigan. This is where he spent most of his time these days. There were a few friends at his table and he had just finished his third Scotch and could feel the booze. He was explaining about his next big scam that would bring the state around twenty million dollars for some needless research project. He would get fifteen percent—three million—of the twenty million for himself just for bringing home the bacon!

Long ago he had lost his integrity, his morals and his interest in serving the people of Michigan. He had also lost his wife and his family and now lived just to scam money out of the federal government and take a bunch for himself. He had a couple personal bodyguards that hung around with him to keep the public off his back. They sat off to the side, each smoking a big cigar and watching the ball game on TV.

The Plan called for the use of four Special Forces men to help with the pickup. Mike Nelson, Frank Mullin, and Norm Rudy, all trained Special Forces guys, were seated in the restaurant so they could watch Senator Henry in the wall mirror. They had finished eating long ago and they were waiting for Henry to hit the road. Outside the restaurant the fourth Special Forces man was on surveillance.

Frank said, "We need to make sure those

bodyguards watching TV do not get in the car with Henry, so we will take them out before they get near their car with our Taser guns."

Norm nodded, adding, "We will use our car to transport Henry to the private airstrip where Rock is with our plane."

Rock had checked the weather, and it was going to be a moonlight night with no wind. Getting into Long Lake by the camp was going to be okay. The plane was the Cessna Amphibian 206, so if the weather broke bad they could get into the Florence airport on wheels and stay until daylight.

Mike spoke up and pointed into the bar. "Henry is leaving. Let's move it."

Henry was through the door before the first bodyguard showed up, and when the guard went into the entryway, Norm touched the 200 volt Taser gun to his back. Mike grabbed him, pulled him out onto the walkway, and dropped him.

Immediately the other guard stepped outside and saw his partner piled up on the concrete. Stepping quickly over to him he knelt down and spoke to him. Norm pushed the 200 volt Taser gun to the man's neck and let it go, dropping him on top of his partner. Working through the jacket of the last guard, Frank found the car keys.

Norm and Frank rushed to the car where Henry was trying to open the door. Rather than stick to the original idea, Norm pushed Henry into the rear seat of the man's own car, after giving him a jolt with the Taser. Frank got up front and started up the car, driving instantly out of the parking lot. No one had left the bar.

Norm followed Frank down the road a couple miles and then the Henry car was parked back in an old grassy road out of view of the highway. Frank, Norm, Mike, and the other Special Forces surveillance man, along with Henry, continued on to the grass strip where Rock and the plane were sitting.

10

After three weeks there were six losers in the Pentoga Swamp Compound, all safe and sound, though angry. No way out, no one coming in, no TV, no newspapers, not anything but isolation for them.

The news media was having a heyday with the disappearance of the crooks. There was lots of speculation about the similarities of each of the missing: e.g. long term politicians with lots of greed who were behind the creation of lots of bad regulations that caused businesses to close and many people to lose their jobs.

Tom Moss had worked as President of the Central

Bank for Wells Fargo for over a decade. He had put a lot of deals together with big corporations and wealthy CEOs. But more important than the deals was the big money he had made on kickbacks from those deals. Moss was on vacation at a resort in Wisconsin, spending his days on the golf course and his nights in the bar with his wife.

Major Mike Nelson was also staying at the resort and planned to pick up Moss and get him to the Pentoga Compound today.

Out in the parking lot of the lodge was an ambulance with Tim Orr, a Special Forces team member working for Mike. At the moment, Moss was walking towards the lodge with another high roller, talking as they walked. Mike walked alongside him, his right hand inside his coat, which showed a small bulge on the right side where a loaded 3-D tranquilizer handgun was holstered. Tim Orr was moving slowly towards Mike with the ambulance.

Mike pulled the trigger on the 3-D, sending a load of dope into Moss's rear end with the gun. Moss collapsed on the tar driveway and all those around him stopped. Out of the ambulance stepped Tim with his medical uniform on.

Tim said, "Please step aside and let me examine this guy."

He placed his stethoscope on Moss. "This guy is having a heart attack. He needs to get to the hospital immediately. Help me load him up."

Fifteen minutes later Moss was stretched out in the back of the 206 amphibian flying off the runway heading for Pentoga.

11

One of the Bell 430 copters, trimmed out with Medivac stickers, had just landed on top the Riverton Enterprise building in Riverton, New Jersey.

The president of RE Inc., was Eric Anderson. He had taken over the business after his dad died six years ago and the business was in trouble financially. Eric was an artist at faking the books. He had kited more than thirty million dollars from other investments and was living it up as those other companies were dying.

More than twelve thousand people had been laid off. They had lost their retirement, their insurance, and most of them were now still unemployed. He had no concern for them. It was not his problem that employees who had been part of the Riverton Enterprise companies were now broke and their lives messed up.

Doug Mason, one of the team members from Mike's Special Forces, was sitting in the Riverton lunchroom, dressed in full corporate suit and tie. There were three other Special Forces members in the Riverton lunchroom at different tables. The Special Forces research group had given Doug information about one of Eric's losing companies. Doug walked over to the table where Eric was eating and introduced himself as an attorney working for one of the laid off employees.

Doug said, "Mr. Anderson, I have some information to share with you that you will be very interested in hearing. There is some real money involved. Could I see you in your office after lunch?"

Eric seemed irritated, but only said, "It better be important. I will see you in my office, suite 921, in thirty minutes."

Doug said, "Thanks," and walked away down the hall. He radioed Jim, the pilot of the copter 430 that was sitting on the roof of the building, and told him the plan was on.

Thirty minutes later, Eric Anderson walked into his office and told the office girl that a Mr. Doug Mason would be coming in for a short meeting and to bring him straight in when he arrived. Mason walked into the office and shook hands with Eric, while compressing a soft tranquilizer needle into his hand. Within ten seconds Eric collapsed in his arms.

Mason radioed his Special Forces men standing outside the office door and told them to come on in and pick up Anderson. Mr. Anderson looked like he was having a heart attack. Two of the Special Forces team members dressed up in medical uniforms walked into the office. They told the office girl that they had just received a 911 call that Eric Anderson was sick and needed some help.

Forty minutes later, Eric Anderson was in the Citation Jet piloted by Rock Smith, headed for the Pentoga Compound with a stop at the Iron Mountain, Michigan, airport. Soon after the sun went down, Anderson arrived by float plane at the compound.

Jack Martin had long been recognized as the

authority on EPA regulations in the Upper Midwest. He chaired a board that would determine what permits would or would not be issued. He was tired of working with the Minnesota Governor, who was requesting permits to open up thousands of acres of wilderness land in Northern Minnesota.

In 2009, a mining company had uncovered millions of tons of copper and nickel below the surface around the town of Ely, Minnesota. That area had once been a big mining area, but many years ago the mining had run out and the towns were kept open with tourism. With the present economy, these towns were all closing up and homes and business were being abandoned. Martin's board had told the Governor that they would not provide the permits and that plenty of copper and nickel were coming in from South America.

The government officials in northern Michigan had recently requested permits to open up a large area. Recent diggings from mining companies in the winter of 2010 had shown billions of dollars of copper below the surface and they were immediately available for mining the copper. This work would employ thousands of workers in an area with over twenty percent unemployment. Jack Martin's board gave the same message to these government officials and local town boards. There was no need to use our resources when others could be obtained from South America.

Jack Martin had a new twin engine airplane and a big home in Florida. Neither of these could be purchased with his annual salary of ninety thousand dollars. Many investigations had been conducted about Jack's resources, but they always resulted in a dead end. It was obvious that he was getting large financial kickbacks from the South American mining companies to buy from them and not allow any new mining to happen in the U.S.

At the moment, Jack was on a fishing trip in Northern Minnesota at a small town on Leech Lake. He was staying in an upscale resort called Trapper's Landing. Nothing was too good for Jack Martin.

Mike Nelsen was also staying at Trapper's Landing Resort along with two other Special Forces men working for him. Martin had just finished his dinner and was sitting in front of a large stone fireplace having an after-dinner drink.

Mike Nelsen walked into the bar and asked if anyone in the bar would like a plane ride to see the four hundred seventy thousand acre lake from the air. The plane was docked out front of the bar and the big sign on the plane showed the name of Trapper's Landing Tours. There were no N-numbers on the plane.

Mike explained that he still had a few seats left and the ride would be about thirty minutes. He walked over by the fireplace and started visiting with two fishermen (Special Forces Men) sitting there and then Mike asked, "What do you think, guys, how about a short ride to see the entire lake?"

He walked over to Jack Martin and said, "Get you back here in half an hour. Bring along your drink."

Martin said. "Well, that sounds like a good idea." He asked his friend next to him, "How about a ride?" He got a yes and they both got up and walked to the bar door and out to the float plane.

The two Special Forces contract men working for Mike were already in the plane, as was Rock Smith, the pilot. Martin and his friend, an EPA board member along on the fishing trip, got buckled in and they were off the water in ten minutes.

They were settled into the Pentoga Compound two hours later.

12

After a month of missing politicians, bankers, and CEOs, the media slowed down its coverage and went back to the normal news output. Rock, Norm and Frank talked about this with Mike Nelson.

Norm said, "We need to pick up some more losers and keep this issue alive."

Frank's comment was, "Let's find a person that is putting money into the scams, someone who is responsible for killing our America." The discussion continued about who would be a good candidate for the next pickup.

Done with the Talking

Rock said, "How about this guy Boris who is breaking all the countries financially. The jerk wants to make our country like Greece, where all the people are attached to the government for food."

So the planning began: to locate, pick up, and get John Boris to the Pentoga Swamp.

Now everything was ready. Norm Rudy remained at Bruce Crossing and Frank Mullin remained at the Pentoga Compound. Rock and Mike's team flew into St. Paul, Minnesota's downtown airport in the 206 amphibian where Rock's leased Citation Eagle jet was parked.

The Eagle had been gassed and ready for departure. It had also been equipped with every possible piece of war equipment that Mike felt necessary to get the job done.

There were a total of eight guys now in the Eagle, including Rock Smith. These guys were all Special Forces trained and experienced. The Citation lifted off the short runway next to the Mississippi River in downtown St. Paul. The weather was clear and stable as Rock cleared the tower for runway 310. He set a heading of 093 degrees and made a scheduled stop in Maine, before leaving U.S. airspace for Italy.

The Cessna Citation Eagle touched down on the long ten thousand foot runway in Catanzaro, Italy. It was just after 19:00 hours and the rain was coming down in a drizzle, making it hard to see at one hundred and forty miles per hour. But Rock Smith had lots of time in F-18s and this was just another day in his office.

The plane rolled slowly and went off ramp towards the dock area. Rock parked the plane and immediately the custom agents appeared at the door. The paperwork had all been handled and the eight men, all in slick business suits, waited for the agent. All questions were answered and the passports were signed, leaving the men still sitting in the plane as the custom agents made their exit.

Mike Nelson, the commander of the Special Forces men was a lean faced man with graying hair. He gave the impression that he was all business, yet gave out a confident feeling to others. He had spent eight years in Special Forces in Iraq and Afghanistan and was a natural leader of the group.

All members of International Special Forces were trained Delta Force Combat Troops. They had all served lots of time on foreign soil, defending the good old U.S.A. in recent years. Each member had signed up to defend the U.S. Constitution, yet their government continued to dismember the elements under that constitution, and greed, lying, and general corruption remained in full force. These Delta Force Combat GIs resigned from the service, going home disillusioned and burned out after serving in the U.S. Special Forces.

A few months after leaving the service each discharged Delta Force GIs received a letter inviting them to join the ISF. The members were living around the world and contacted only when there was a need to make changes. Mike had contacted Captain Jim Donavan, a buddy who was living in Italy, to assist in the capture of Boris.

Mike's team left the plane at the Catanzaro Airport around 20:00 hours and Rock stayed with the Citation.

Crotone, Italy, was a small town on the Mediterranean Sea, thirty-five miles from the airport.

The town was in a deeply wooded area and remote, with very few homes. This was not a fishing village or tourist town, but a remote location for elite people who had lots of money. Major security took lots of cash, and John Boris had it. His security included over fifty trained combat troops and millions of dollars of electronic surveillance equipment, including satellite. Hiding out had long been an issue for Boris. Many people had tried to take him out, and they were all dead. He lived in a fortress of granite more than five stories high and covering four acres.

Donavan had rented Land Cruisers for the group and they were now fifteen miles northwest, moving along the sea twenty miles south of Crotone. The ride was quiet, with little traffic and little talking in the cruisers. This was not the team's first rodeo, and although there was a great sense of urgency to get the job done, there was no hurry. The team was confident, but aware that a lot of things needed to work, which meant that errors and the unexpected could and probably would, happen.

At 21:40 hours Mike made a call to Jim Donavan, who had been in the area for the past week, confirming that he had made it and was about to reach the rendezvous location. Jim confirmed and contact ceased.

The rendezvous location had been handpicked to allow for the hiding of the Land Cruisers nearby. The cruisers were needed to get back to the airport with Mike's team and John Boris. The location required that the team be far enough from the estate and Crotone to stop any surveillance contact by Boris. Donavan had confirmed that Boris was at home at this time.

The plan was set.

13

Pulling into the rendezvous spot, the cruisers stopped and Mike's crew quickly unloaded and walked toward the sea. Donavan was there to meet Mike and with a handshake, they moved to the shoreline. The cruisers were parked in the woods out of sight of the road and under some large trees. There were nine Special Forces men now on the beach, along with eight Seabob U.S. 7s and one Seabob U.S. 8 that Donavan had secured. The Seabob U.S. 8 was a double occupancy unit that would provide a seat for Boris on the return trip.

The Seabobs allowed for silent underwater propulsion. They were high-tech underwater machines developed by the U.S. Field Operations. They could run at thirty miles per hour for four hours. Each Seabob had closed Draegar Lar V "rebreathing" devices that stopped all bubbles going to the surface. Each Seabob had DSI M48 Super masks that allowed team communications underwater. Each member had been trained by U.S. Army's Special Forces Combat Diver Qualification Courses in Florida.

In each Seabob 7 there were two MP40 guns, each with one hundred rounds of ammo and one grease machine gun M-3. The pack for each member held a Glock handgun, 45 caliber, and fifty rounds of ammo, four IEDs, and two days of dried food, along with two quarts of water. Each Seabob member also had scopes on their MP40 that showed heat sensors and night vision, and a hand held air pressured gun to send out darts filled with knock-out juice. The Seabob 8 held two LaRus Sniper rifles along with two hundred rounds of ammo. There was a small Browns Gas cutting torch ready for use. This torch could cut stone, metal, plastic, brick and could work underwater.

Mike said, "Good place to start a war."

No one commented.

It took less than ten minutes to get off shore. Soon the team was approaching the shoreline in front of the Boris estate. There were lights from the house that reflected across the water and everyone was careful to not get near the surface as they moved along the shore. On the far north edge of the property there was a large drainage culvert. The architect who had remodeled the place had been helpful in providing all details about the estate. Donavan was leading and looking for the culvert.

Donavan said, "I found the drainage culvert, and it has one inch mesh covering the end. Seabob 8, come up front and cut this mesh open."

"Roger that, Donavan."

Seabob 8 moved up through the other Seabobs alongside of Jim Donavan, took out the Browns Gas torch and struck the igniter. The flame immediately showed up. Within five minutes a large 6x6 foot hole had been cut, allowing the Seabobs to enter the culvert.

"So far so good," commented Jim.

Moving slowly up into the drainage culvert, they

came up to the home's foundation. Team members looked again at the drawings on the water screen of the home's design. The foundation was covered with magnesium, set into concrete. This would normally have stopped any access through the foundation. However, the Browns Gas, which is used to cut all metal, cement, wood, and plastic, soon cut though the cement and the magnesium.

Browns Gas is made by taking the hydrogen out of water, resulting in a flame that does not cut with temperature, but by chemically changing the elements of cement and metal into a liquid. Soon the foundation and metal were pulled away, allowing the men to swim under the home. They had three hours until daylight which should be adequate to get the job done.

The elevator on the west end of the house went down to the basement level and they were now alongside that shaft. Using the heat sensors, they did not find anyone inside the two foot thick elevator walls or near the door. All members had removed most of their underwater gear, yet they did have communication and all the hardware to keep them alive. The Browns Gas machine was now attached to a pack and was being used to cut a hole through the elevator wall.

Once inside the elevator, seven members went to the top floor where Boris slept, leaving two members to control the elevator and keep the escape route open. Checking the heat sensors for guards on the top floor, they found six locations where there were live bodies stationed. Six bodies and seven Special Forces guys. Mike assigned each member to a specific target.

The door was opened and instantly the first guard was hit with a shot from a 3-D tranquilizer handgun. Around the corner to the left, the heat sensors showed two guards within fifty feet, one on the left and one on the right side of the hallway. Mike's assigned men took each one of these out. Four team members stepped out into the hall surprising the two guards, who realized what was going on too late to react. They both fell off their chairs within ten seconds from the 3-D handguns and lay quiet.

Boris's bedroom was another sixty feet down the hall and to the right. Four members moved down towards the bedroom and three remained to see that none of the sleeping guards woke up. The shot from the 3-D should keep them quiet for forty-five minutes, but you never know.

Done with the Talking

There were two more guards in front of the Boris door. These were put to sleep immediately by the Special Forces men. Mike opened the bedroom door and stepped into the room. John Boris was sitting up in bed, reading. His mouth dropped open and his eyes showed panic, but not for long, as Mike shot him with a good dose of knock-out juice from his 3-D handgun.

Two of the Special Forces guys picked him up and put him in a sling that held his body. The sling wrapped around Mike's back. Mike touched the mike fastened to his collar and gave all the members notice that they had Boris and were moving back to the elevator. Each member gave him a clear click and there were seven clicks. A few minutes later all Special Forces members had stepped outside the elevator opening and were putting back on their water gear. The elevator wall cut out was welded back in place. It all seemed too perfect.

14

Rock had a thirty mile per hour wind behind his back as the Citation Eagle nosed toward Newfoundland at four hundred and twenty knots ground speed. The trip back was uneventful, and Boris was at twenty-two thousand feet before he woke up.

Mike leaned over and spoke to him. "How are you feeling? Can I get you anything to drink?"

Boris did not respond, but his eyes told the story of fear.

It was a day later as the Cessna 206 came in over Long Lake. The stars were bright, but there was not much moonlight, though enough to ensure an easy landing. Rock pulled on twenty degree flaps and started his descent, circling the lake out front of the compound. He passed over the lake at five hundred feet to see if any debris was floating in the water and then circled back around.

Putting on another ten degrees flaps, he started his final approach. He checked to see if the gear lights were on, showing that the wheels were pulled up into the floats, and added some trim. The plane settled easily on the water. Pulling back on the gas and bringing the plane to an idle, he taxied over near the compound. There was no dock available, but help was there to stabilize the plane as it mushed up on the weeds.

The cool fall air showed signs of winter coming on. The trees were changing color and the sky over Rudy's cabin seemed full of waterfowl heading south from the Arctic. The snow in the U.P. usually started in mid November and stayed until mid April. The lake effect from Lake Superior produced over three hundred inches of snow that was found in the hills and all the roads except for state and federal were closed. All the county roads remained as snowmobile trails during the winter months. It was time to start stock-piling gas, food, and other supplies for the Pentoga Compound.

It was important that no sign of traffic showed up on the lake or in the woods. No snow skis could be used on the airplanes to take in people or get them out, because the skis would leave ruts on the snow that could be seen by planes or satellite. No snowmobiles could be used either, since they also left trails behind.

Since Frank Mullin was responsible for the caretaking of the compound, these concerns belonged to him. Dozens of vendors were contacted that would provide food and gas. All this would be unloaded at Moose Creek in Bruce Crossing. The large heated shop south of the old cabin was perfect for this. The food was all purchased using several company names and tax numbers, and all the supplies were picked up directly from the vendors.

The purchasing should be complete by the end of October. The copters would then take these items into the compound at night, unload them, and return back to Moose Creek.

Several weeks had passed and the media was

going crazy. The federal government was on top alert across America; after all, Boris had been calling the shots on the demise of the U.S.A.

Dozens of senators and representatives were troubled. Each of them had received millions of dollars from Boris to vote on issues that would bring more unemployment and more uncertainty for the young and old. America was scheduled to go broke like many countries in Europe. When they went broke, new money was printed and handed out to banks to use in the market place. This money was controlled by Boris. His dream was to take out the biggest trophy of all – the U.S.A.

The Special Forces teams continued to find and capture crooked politicians, bankers, and CEOs and bring them to the compound. There were now more than one hundred and forty crooks sleeping in the swamp compound. There were more than seventy Special Forces members involved in the plan. Mike Nelson's team of ten remained at the Pentoga compound. The others, who held regular jobs across America, were on alert and waiting for a call from Mike.

Congress was unable to function, as it could not

get enough members to complete a vote on spending more money. The public was grinning about the fact that no money was being printed, no money was buying out failed businesses and no money was being used to fund green industries. More than one hundred and twenty statesmen had resigned for fear that they would be the next to disappear from the scene.

The night was stormy, with high winds and pouring rain. The Pentoga Compound was warm and each prisoner was locked in their bedroom. The windowless bedrooms had one small cot and a small commode. A sink was available to brush their teeth and wash up. No showers existed.

The security provided by Special Forces members remained on high alert. Motion sensors surrounded the compound, along with numerous traps and pits, should any one find their way into the area around the buildings. The biggest concern was identification from satellites that would pick up motion, lights, or any changes in the area. The building had been sealed to stop heat sensors from working by using titanium plating on the outside of all structures. But a perfect plan does not make all things safe. The bank of TVs used to observe the grounds was monitored twenty-four hours a day.

Suddenly a Pentoga guard pushed an alert button that covered a small strip of the creek shoreline one thousand yards to the north. There was some movement, as well as heat identification from the swamp grass area. No visual contact had been made, but the sensors were showing human signals, not animal. Immediately Mike assigned three Special Forces men to search out the problem.

15

While Frank Mullin remained at the Pentoga Compound as controller of the overall operation, Norm had been busy with following the expenses and dealing with the bank in Platteville, Wisconsin. FRN, Inc. had burned through almost eighty-three million dollars and there was still two hundred million in the shop at Bruce Crossing. He remained in his cabin at Bruce Crossing and had been left with the responsibility of handling the money for the company. He still drove his old pickup, still lived in the run down cabin, and spent his days on his computers working on managing the funds needed to handle the Swamp Operation.

Meanwhile, Rock Smith continued to live in his cabin in Montana and did some local flying and instruction at the airport. His cabin was also tied into the Pentoga and Bruce Crossing offices. His Cessna 206 amphibian was hangared at the airport, out of sight most of the time. Most of Rock's flying was at night when he was working for RFN, Inc.

Since he had years of experience hunting in the mountains of Montana, he decided to see if he could break into the security of the Pentoga Compound. If he could do it, so could others. He was a pilot, not a Special Forces guy, but he had spent lots of time in the bush.

It was 03:00 hours, and the smell of the swamp muck, the attacks of mosquitoes getting in under the bug mask, and the two-mile crawl up along the Pentoga Creek gave Rock a challenge. He did not have any weapons except his 9mm automatic pistol strapped to his side. He did have his heat sensor and motion detector scope. He was determined to check out the security on the compound.

His GPS showed he was within fifteen hundred feet of the buildings, and he was aware that he could be getting picked up by the sensors that covered every inch of space within the fifteen hundred foot circumferences of the place. What he did not know was whether the monitors, or those doing the monitoring, were doing their job.

He was now within seven hundred feet of the compound, and yet there was no evidence that anyone had spotted him. He remained still for five minutes, continuing to use his scope, searching ahead of him for any sign. He crept slowly forward, pushing the tall swamp grass aside with his face, stopping often to listen. He was now within five hundred feet of the compound, and he did not think he had been detected.

Just as the swamp grass parted and he pushed ahead, he saw a red dot against the shiny stems of grass. He froze in position, recognizing the laser light coming from his right side off to the rear.

"Do not move! Do not turn your head! Lay flat on the grass with your face down!" said a deep voice.

Rock could hear the quiet footsteps as someone moved through the grass; he could hear the swish of the swamp grass brushing against cotton cloth moving closer. The feeling of the cold steel of a rifle barrel against his neck was real. He lay dead still.

Finally the voice said, "Sit up and turn around."

Rock slowly came to a sitting position and said, "Can I remove my bug mask?"

The answer was, "Very slowly and with only one hand."

Rock pulled away his mask and said, "I am Captain Rock Smith, one of the owners of the Swamp Compound."

Tim Short, one of the men Mike Nelson had asked to check out the person showing up on the sensors, said, "Stand up, turn around, and put up your hands. I don't care who you are. You are in trouble."

Tim Short and the others had moved to the rear of Rock as he had been crawling along the creek and had approached him from the rear. While Rock was focused on what was ahead of him, they were observing him in their scopes from the rear. Tim placed handcuffs on Rock and the four of them walked onto the compound.

Mike Nelson met Rock at the door. "Good job, guys. Meet one of your bosses," he said.

As Mike and Rock had a cup of coffee, Rock said, "I had to find out for myself if the security on this place was perfect and I am now satisfied that we are safe."

16

The winter had come and gone, grass was turning green at Bruce Crossing, and almost a year had passed since the start of Operation Pentoga. Most of the people being held had been in place for six months. The country was in chaos.

Norm Rudy, Frank Mullin and Rock Smith were sitting on the deck with Mike Nelson, who was visiting, talking about the next phase of the Pentoga Plan. The summer winds were blowing off Moose Creek, giving up a fishy smell and the mosquitoes were not too bad on the deck with the breeze blowing.

Mike said, "The compound has been filled with these crooks for six months. They have had lots of isolation, lots of time to think. So what should be done?"

Norm said, "The public needs to know they are still alive. They need to know the truth about each of these jerks."

Frank commented, "We need to find out from each one what they have done with all the money they stole and how they stole it."

"I would like Boris to write a press release about his dream of bringing the U.S. to its knees and how he would benefit from that," said Norm.

"Starting tomorrow, let's interview each one of them starting with Boris. Let's meet with them in their rooms and if they ask what we intend to do with them in the future, just say that will depend on the interviews and leave it at that," said Frank.

Norm Rudy sat across the small table from Boris. A year had passed, but Rudy's disposition remained the same. His thick shoulders, large muscled arms and hands leaned against the broken, unfinished table. Norm's hair was shiny black and combed to perfection. His green eyes held Boris's attention with a piercing look. There was nothing coming back from those eyes, as they focused directly on the man.

After five silent minutes he said, "Boris, I have not spoken to you for almost five months and I am not excited about our visit here this morning. I am sure you want to know what is in your future. I can tell you this. The answers to the questions I ask you will determine your future."

Boris was leaning back in the cloth lawn chair on the other side of the table. He was not looking at Norm. Rather, his eyes seem attached to the ceiling of his room. His persona was one of indifference, one of lost hope and despair. His grey shaggy hair covered his shoulders and his beard hung to his chest. Although the room had running water, a sink and clean towels each day, it looked like the last time he washed was weeks ago. His bed sheets had not been changed for a month. Here was one of the wealthiest men in the world, yet he was emotionally broken and ready to touch another human, ready to hear a voice, and hoping someone cared.

Norm said, "I want you to tell me about your life

as a young boy, about your childhood, about your family."

A video camera was attached to Norm Rudy's jacket and had been turned on before he entered the room. For a few minutes Boris remained quiet, almost like he had not heard the command.

Then he said, "I grew up in the house that you broke into. I lived in that home as far back as I can remember. I was an only child and I spent most of my childhood years with my mother. My early memories of my father were during the war with Hitler.

When I was five, Hitler was in our house for several days working with my father and several others. I had a German Shepherd pup that was always chewing on everything. During the meeting in the large office, my pup found Hitler's boots in the entry way and spent considerable time chewing on them. He was still chewing on them when Hitler decided to leave for his cottage. When he saw what the pup had done, he pulled a knife from his sleeve, reached down, and picked up the pup and slit its throat and just dropped it back on the hardwood floor.

My dad was standing nearby and watched this

happen. All he did was ask the butler to remove the dog. He never once looked at me. It was like I never existed for my father. As I grew older I found out that the plan for Hitler's takeover of Germany and his plan for a super race were put together in our home. I was nine years old when I found out that my father had been killed in Germany.

My parent's families had lived in the Crotone area for centuries. They had always been very wealthy and powerful people. As I grew older and went to college, my life was totally planned for me – where I went, who I met, what I wore, and what schooling I took. I did not meet any one that was not a communist until I was thirty years old.

My intent from high school on was to the rule the world, not through war, but by the use of power and money. To control the world it was necessary to undo the governments that had been installed in Europe, by breaking the economy and breaking the spirit of the people. When they are hungry and desperate they can be managed. They must be down and out before they will listen.

My family has spent over one hundred years breaking up and controlling the governments of Europe. The foundations for Russia and the enormous countries around Russia have all run under the communist program. Millions have died and millions more will die before I can get this old world to shape up.

I am working with hundreds of U.S. politicians, bankers, and others to bring down the U.S. and turn it into a communist country, and it seems to be going well." Boris stopped talking and sat in the lawn chair looking across the table at Norm.

"Would you care to name those people that are working with you?" asked Norm. There was a long silence in the room as Boris dropped his head, looking at the worn wooden floor.

"How long have I been here?" he asked.

"Almost five months," Norm answered. Another long quiet period occurred and neither of them spoke.

Finally Boris said, "What are you going to do with me?"

"That depends on you," said Norm. "If you do

not cooperate with us, you could spend the rest of your life in this room. You are in a location that defies finding by the U.S. government. You will recall from when we picked you up that we're not a cowboy operation, but are very well financed and have our own Special Forces. You are very likely going to die here if you do not do what we ask. In fact, if I am not happy with the information I get today, I will see you in another four months. It's up to you," said Norm.

"So what exactly do you want from me today?" asked Boris.

Norm pulled out a tablet from his brief case and handed it across the table along with several pens. "I want the names of all the government people you are working with to bring down the U.S. government and I want you to write out what specific plans are in progress at this moment. I will be back here in two hours to see how you are doing. Remember what I said. If you do not have the information on the pads in front of you when I return I will see you in another four months and maybe then you will work with me."

The door closed softly as Norm walked out. The

one 40-watt light bulb that hung from the ceiling in Boris's room did not dispel the gloom. Boris sat slumped over in his lawn chair watching a couple ants move on the dirty floor. His mind was now alert and even at age seventy-seven his thinking was clear. For the first time in his life he was not in control of his plan to take over the world.

What was the U.S. President doing to him? Surely with all his power and money he should have found him by now. What was holding up his rescue? His first reaction was to blow off the request to name all the people working with him, to shut down any attempt from this guy Norm to explain his plans for the future.

He had two hours to get the work done before the guy came back. Thinking about it, he became very angry and stomped his feet as he got up to walk around the small room. He rubbed his face and pressed down his long hair. His hands kept stroking his long shaggy beard. He could not believe that the guy would walk out of his room and leave him here for the next four months.

Yet, it had been almost five months before they had made this first contact and he was almost crazy with isolation. He continued to wring his hands in despair. What should he do? Could he give him made-up names? Should he not do anything? What were they going to do with him anyway, even if he gave up the information?

With tears in his eyes, he began writing down names of government people, industry CEOs, trade union leaders and those in the President's office. He was running out of time and was not finished with outlining his plans to break the economy of the U.S. when he heard the latch on his door lift and saw the door opening.

Norm did not look at Boris until he was seated across from him. He could see writing on the yellow tablet and just watched as Boris continued his scratching on the paper. Ten minutes passed before Boris pushed the tablet across the rough table top over to him. Boris laid down his pen and leaned back, not saying a word.

Norm said, "John, what you have there had better be the truth. Now here is what is going to happen. You are being taped on video as we speak. You will now introduce yourself and tell the world that you are well and safe and that you have a message for them. Then you will start reading the names of all the people on your paper and then you will explain what they have been doing to help in the destruction of the U.S. economy. When this has been done, you will explain the current plan going on across the country to bring it all down.

Do you understand me? Your picture and confession will be on CNN by nightfall today. Do you understand what you are going to do and what will happen to the information? At the end of your confession I may ask you to clarify some things and to answer a few questions.

Now sit back and look across the table at me. The lens of the video camera is here on my shirt, so look directly into the lens when you speak. I am not in a hurry – take as much time as you need to finish the task. Remember, your future depends on how well you do this next hour."

It was over two hours later before John Boris stopped reeling off his information. It sounded too real to be just made up and the details were so involved that Norm could hardly believe what he was hearing.

Finally, Boris just stopped speaking and looked into those green eyes of Norm's. Not even contempt showed on Norm's face, and the deadpan eyes that had seen and heard too much for his young years were unreadable.

Reaching across the table Norm picked up the tablet and walked out of the room, leaving Boris looking exhausted.

17

Mike Nelson and his team of Special Forces were handed the edited videos by Rock Smith.

Rock said, "The information is set up for five TV specials over the next ten days. Whatever you need to do to sanitize these tapes, do it. It is your responsibility to make sure that they cannot be traced to anyone. Use your underground connections to see that these are given to CNN, FOX, and the other major TV stations immediately."

The Fox news was on across America. It was 18:00 hours and O'Reilly was just opening his segment on world news. All of a sudden, a Special News Bulletin came over the screen. A video was playing, showing John Boris, the man who had been missing for the past several months. Boris introduced himself and told what he was about to do. He explained that he had been treated well and all the information he was about to share with the world was true.

The newscast lasted for thirty minutes and during this time more than sixty specific names were given out, the details on how they had worked to destroy the U.S., and how much money each had received for their work was all explained very clearly. At the end of the tape Boris told the watchers that four additional tapes would be forthcoming in the next several days. Dozens of additional names of powerful people would be included in these future tapes.

The tape went off the air. Americans across the country were astounded that people they knew – union officials, corporate leaders, and many state and federal politicians – had been named.

By the next morning, chaos reigned across the country. The legal beagles were on it big time. The press was trying to schedule meetings with the people whose names had been given, while newspapers reported the details of the tapes and asked for responses from those named individuals. There was a hush in the Left Media. They were not sure if or when some of them would be named in the plot to take down America. Hundreds of CEOs went on vacation to avoid the press and the federal government began coming unglued. The Vice President was in the hospital and not to be disturbed, although his name had not been mentioned by Boris.

Within three days the media was all over it, saying that the old bearded guy that had made those accusations was not Boris, but just an old man from the drug world. Immediately, the Power Players picked up on that and made discrediting statements in interviews. The Democratic Party was having a field day with the dumb remarks made in the video.

Four days after the video had aired, a bulletin came up on screens during the morning news on TV. There was a second video showing the old bearded man, and this time the message started out with, "Maybe the last time I visited with you, you thought I was not John Boris. Today I will share a little information about myself."

He proceeded to tell about his childhood, his

years living with the wealthy and powerful, about his family who was part of the German planning with Hitler. He spoke about his involvement in the demise of several countries in Europe and just who he had worked with in those countries. He then proceeded to list names and tell about the help he had received from those people.

Again the public was dumfounded at getting the specific names of those who had helped to create unemployment, those who had helped stop the drilling of the oil wells, and those who had passed dozens of regulations to stop mining and the lumber industry. The video went off the air with John saying, "See you soon."

Two additional tapes played over the next week and dozens of names were given out. The news was showing countless suicides, CEOs losing their positions, politicians resigning, and union leaders being sued by the public for misuse of funds.

But it was not over yet.

The final video showed up on a Monday morning. This time Boris talked only about the U.S. President. He said, "This man is truly a communist and will not be satisfied until the country goes broke. His plan and mine is to take over the American economy and see that everyone works for the government."

With that, he signed off by saying he was sorry that he was now unable to complete his work.

18

The U.S. Department of Homeland Security was on an all-out search for the location of the missing people. The satellites were ordered to check out every square mile of the U.S. All satellites that were normally used for TV, businesses, and foreign countries were taken over by the government to search the earth.

Hundreds of unmanned drones circled the U.S. There was a general consensus that the prisoners were being housed in a wilderness, rather than in an urban location. There would be too much exposure if they were in a city: getting their hostages to the prison, supplying food to them, keeping them well, etc., required complete isolation for those being held.

There were dozens of union bosses now sitting in jail waiting court hearings. Several thousand CEOs of large financial institutions were suspended from work pending investigation. Both the President and Vice-President had resigned, and the Speaker of the House now worked in the Oval Office.

A new election was being scheduled across America for dozens of politicians, a President, and a Vice President. The U.S. Department of Education no longer existed, as many people in that organization had resigned. Most teachers unions had been dissolved and local school boards were now operating schools. Copies of the Ten Commandments hung in the school halls and prayer was back as well. Oil wells were being drilled wherever the land showed oil deposits in America. Oil pipelines were being dug twenty-four hours, seven days a week to deliver the oil to refineries.

Federal and state land was no longer under the DNR or Forest Service. Tens of thousands of government employees were laid off. This land was being sold or left to go wild again. Thousands of regulations and rules were being voted off the books and construction was going big time. The U. S. Constitution was back on track to serve America.

Yet the Pentoga Swamp Compound remained in operation, all of the prisoners still in their rooms.

19

A year and a half had passed and during that year Rock Smith had built a log home on his land in Montana. He had found his old high school sweetheart and was now married. His dark brooding eyes were happy and there was a smile on his face. His wife was expecting a baby in six months and they were both very excited about life. They had joined a small Christian church near the airport and for once in his adult life, Rock felt at home.

Then he received a call from Frank Mullin, asking that they get together back at Pentoga to make decisions about the future of the residents there. The wind was coming out of the west, straight down grass runway 270. The hard surface runway 311 was normally used, but today he decided to go off the grass runway to avoid the strong crosswinds.

Flying amphibian floats made the plane high above the surface and hard to control in strong crosswinds. The grassy runway was sheltered by large trees and underbrush close to the runway, which helped to prevent direct crosswinds but also created stronger down drafts moving across the tree tops and then blowing down to the ground. None of this was unknown by Rock and none of it was a big concern, due to his thousands of hours of flying, but just to be safe he made the choice to head out on 270.

Doing the preflight run-up, he put on twenty degree flaps, ran the engine up to 1700 rpms, checked the mags, set the compass, and checked the seat belt and door locks. It all looked good.

Hitting the mike, he announced, "This is Cessna 4748 Uniform departing on runway 270."

The plane started its roll out and quickly reached forty miles per hour. At that instant, a black Suburban drove out of the trees, moving directly into his path and parked on the grassy strip. Instantly Rock backed off on the throttle and applied the brakes, coming to a stop one hundred feet from the truck.

Out of the truck stepped Zanon and two other guys. They approached the plane from both sides. Zanon walked up to the pilot side and stood next to the pontoon.

Rock opened his window and said "What's up, Zanon?" The tone of his voice was not friendly.

Zanon said, "Get out of the plane, Rock. We need to talk."

Rock's immediate reaction was to run the engine up to 3000 rpms and hit the left brake, doing a spin around and head down wind away from these guys, but he decided to be cool about the visit and find out what it was all about. After pulling out the manifold pressure, he turned off the master, stopping the engine.

He opened the door and stepped down on the float steps onto the float and then off onto the ground next to Zanon. The black Suburban was now moving down the strip towards the plane.

When it stopped, Zanon said, "Get in. We are going for a ride."

Rock moved into the rear door of the waiting truck and sat down beside a bearded giant. The truck moved back around and into the trees from where it had come. Forty-five minutes later, they pulled into a mountain hunting shack that looked like it had been occupied for a while. A large stack of wood and two pickup trucks were parked out front.

Zanon said, "Move off into the cabin, all of you, and let's have a drink."

It had been just over two years since Rock had had that run-in with Zanon when hunting elk and there was something very different about Zanon today. His hair was long and unkept, his long whiskers showed lots of gray, and his clothes were rumpled and dirty. There was a wild look in his eyes, and his mouth was hard.

Zanon said, "Have a seat, Rock, so we can talk. The last time we talked, you said if we ever met again, you would beat me to within an inch of my life. Now I just think you were mad and did not really mean that, so today we are going to start all over. I want you to meet a couple of my employees, Charlie and Storm. I have been telling them about you and our flying days together in the Air Force. By the looks of things out at your house, you have never made a lot of money, but I see you are now married and have a neat little comfortable home for the two of you. So apparently there was nothing found in those records you flew back to Ellsworth, or you would not be living like a pauper out here in the middle of nowhere."

Rock was irritated to find that Zanon had been sneaking around spying on his home and his wife, but did not react, saying only, "You got that right, Zanon – I told you there never was anything in those documents. I live by doing some flying here in the area for farmers and flying for some of those that have emergencies out here. I wish that somehow a guy could make some decent money, but it looks like I would need to move out of this area and find a job someplace else."

"Well, that's why we are here today: to try and give you some business to make some serious money. I would like to talk to you about our business and let you think about it for a couple days before you give me your answer," said Frank Zanon.

Rock said, "Well, let's hear the story."

Frank said to Charlie, "Give him a general overall plan on how he can make some big money and a little bit about how our company works."

Charlie said, "First a little background on Zanon and me. We went to college together before he went into the Air Force and I went to work for his uncle Ray in Chicago, doing books for him. When Zanon got back home a couple years ago, we ran into one another and he was looking for something to do to make a buck. Ray asked him to come to work for him.

Zanon's work is meeting with brokers in South America and other places to set up meetings and locate supplies that need to be hauled into the U.S. The company has grown large, and now Zanon is the boss and Uncle Ray is gone. So Frank and I were talking about someone we could trust to handle and coordinate all the freight by the use of airplanes."

"That's pretty much the story," said Frank Zanon.

Rock decided to ask some general questions.

"How are you fixed for financing to get the work done? Who is doing that work now?"

Zanon said, "We have adequate money to run the company and can pay for whatever equipment is necessary to handle the freight. The last guy that was working for us decided to be the boss and we had to let him go."

Rock said, "It sounds great. So, how about that drink you were talking about? I am interested, but will need to talk with my wife and let you know. I am sure she will be excited about having a little more money for our new baby that is on the way."

"Where were you headed when we stopped you?" Zanon asked.

Rock had anticipated that question and was ready for it. "I was to pick up a family in Butte this afternoon and take them to Mayo Clinic in Minnesota. One of their kids is very sick. So I will get them over there and hang around for a day or two until the kid has had the treatments for cancer and then fly them back here.

When I get back and explain to my wife that I

am taking a flying job with you guys, I am sure it will work out for us. I'm assuming that I would be gone a week or so at a time and then I could spend time here with her? I should be getting on the move shortly. Leave me your phone number and where we can meet to get the details later this week."

They finished up the cocktails and Zanon said, "Well, that sounds great, Rock. Let's get you back to the airport and I will expect to hear from you later in the week."

An hour later Rock Smith was at fifty-five hundred feet heading for Pentoga Swamp to meet with Mullin and Rudy.

20

Rock dropped down for a landing in Fargo and topped off his wing tanks and went to the head. Twenty minutes later, he was up and headed east with the new turbo 206 bound for Florence, Wisconsin. The plane was on automatic pilot and flying at a ground speed of two hundred and twelve miles per hour.

Rock confirmed with Rudy that he had an ETA of 18:00 hours at the Pentoga compound. A couple hours later he could see Long Lake off on the horizon. Easing off on the throttle, he began his approach to the lake. The sun was just starting to drop below the tree line, and his radar showed no other aircraft in the area. Putting on thirty degree flaps, he flew across the lake, checked it out for floating debris, and then returned for a landing.

Norm, Rock, Frank, and Mike headed to the security room off to the left of the compound entry. The discussion included what to do with the prisoners after almost a year. This decision was tabled by Rock, as he proceeded to talk about his meeting with Zanon. Mike was excited about the opportunity to get involved with Zanon's plan. It dealt with bringing in drugs from South America or bringing illegals across the border for sure. There were now seventy Special Forces guys on retainers to work for FRN, Inc., and Mike was in charge of their dispatch.

Four days later, Rock touched down in Rockford, Illinois, in the 206 and taxied up to the terminal marked private. Shutting off the plane, he picked up his bag and exited down the float ladder and headed to the door of the private terminal office. Standing out in the hall was Zanon and his giant gorilla, Charlie.

Zanon said, "Thanks for being on time, Rock. We need to go to my office and give you a briefing. Bring along your pack."

Driving across the city to his office, Zanon began talking about the plans that he wanted Rock to carry out.

Zanon said, "Here is what I have planned for you this week. When we come back to the airport you will see three Citation jets parked in my private hangar. You will meet with the other two pilots for these planes when we get to the office. One of the planes will be yours. We have three loads of freight in Columbia ready to pick up and they are located in three different spots. You will see the site maps in my office and you can work up your flight plans for the three planes. You do not need to know what the freight consists of and are not responsible for loading or unloading anything. You will get your return flight information when you have arrived back in U.S. airspace. Are you clear so far?"

Rock responded, "How do I make some money on this work? I don't care what you are hauling, but I do care about the money I take home."

Zanon said, "I am sure that you will make more money this week than you have ever made before. If all goes well, you will get ten thousand dollars in cash when you return the planes back here to Rockford."

"Sounds good to me. Do you have any co-pilots available to go along?" asked Rock.

"No, you guys are on your own, but you will see that the other pilots are very experienced and easy to work with," answered Zanon.

It was 14:00 hours when the three pilots had completed the flight plans and left the office to head back to the airport. Rock said, "I want to see each of the other jets and do a run-up with each of you as soon as we get there."

He walked through each plane, checking out the instruments and doing an engine run-up with the pilot. He had brought along small time lapse transmitters that he stuck under each co-pilot seat. This would turn on after three hours, allowing Mike Nelson to find out the location of each plane as they showed up on his GPS system back in Pentoga.

Rock and the other pilots flew at twenty-two thousand feet while in U.S airspace and then dropped down below radar just over the Baja Peninsula. Running at forty-five hundred feet, they flew over the ocean heading for Columbia, with GPS headings laid out for the first pickup.

Three hours had passed since leaving Rockford and they were two hundred miles from the first pick up destination. Bill Bruns, one of the other pilots, was assigned to pick up the first load of freight. There was no communication being used to let the freight handlers know an ETA.

Thirty minutes later, Bill eased his plane down onto the forty-five hundred foot hard surface runway. He had done this before, and as the other two planes watched from above, they saw that a perfect landing had been made. Bill was to wait there until he saw the other two planes show up on the return trip.

Rock was the last to land and his expectations were verified once he taxied up to the shack alongside the runway. There were five men waiting for him and he was waved up to the shack and signaled to shut off the engine. He needed gas and they had a large tanker truck standing by, waiting to fill the plane.

The cargo door was opened by Rock and one of the men jumped up into the cargo space and began taking bundles from the men on the ground. Rock spoke to no one – just watched as they completed the loading. He was off the ground in forty minutes and headed back to the second pickup area.

As he approached, he could see the other pilot circling around above that site, waiting for Rock to make visual contact. After Bill Bruns was picked up at the first pickup area, they took a heading of 280 degrees and remained at forty-five hundred feet until they were close to U.S. airspace.

They then took the planes up to twenty-eight thousand feet and headed northeast on a 070 degree heading. They cleared customs in the air and reported that they were going to land at U.S. Customs in Fargo, North Dakota. They filed their flight plans, put the planes on auto pilot, and sat back.

They were carrying over three thousand pounds of drugs in each plane and bucking a head wind of thirty-four miles per hour. With that much weight and the wind, the plane ran at three hundred and sixty miles per hour ground speed.

As the planes approached Fargo, it was now 17:00 hours – four hours before ETA showed on the flight plan. They dropped below radar coverage to twenty-five hundred feet and headed to the hard surface runway in Sioux Narrows, Ontario, Canada. The one hundred and twenty air miles were eaten up in thirty minutes, and Bill Bruns circled over Lake of the Woods using a long approach to the airstrip.

The strip was running west at 260 degrees, with the runway rising up directly away from the lake toward the east with a twenty degree up-slant, so the plane would land going uphill. With the heavy weight on board, Bill kept the airspeed at one hundred and fifteen miles per hour and touched down on the runway just past the water's edge.

The airport had been built primarily for large planes used to fly tourists to the Arctic and had served lots of 727 jets. There was six thousand five hundred feet of hard concrete, and it was big enough to handle the Citations. This airport had little use, since the Canadian tourism business had declined substantially over the past few years. It was not manned, but did have runway lights in operation.

Soon all three planes were safely on the ground with lights and engines off.

The small Indian village a mile to the south of

the airport provided the help to unload the freight into a couple of large enclosed trucks. Rock and Bill Bruns had the responsibility of assisting with the transporting of the freight until it was safely across into the U.S. One pilot remained with the planes and had to get them ready for departure as soon as the guys returned.

The Rainy River runs east and west, providing the border between the U.S. and Canada. The river runs from Fort Frances, Canada, to Baudette, Minnesota. It is a quiet, five hundred foot wide river with treed banks. Canada has over four thousand miles of unguarded border, so it is not a problem to move drugs from Canada into the U.S. by boating the freight across the river. Highway 71 goes from Sioux Falls, Canada, to the Rainy River about thirty miles to the south.

Rock said, "How long will it take to get to the drop off spot and get unloaded? I would like to get back to the planes and get back to Illinois yet tonight."

Big George, one of the drivers, said, "We should have you back up here at the airport within two hours, depending on if the boat is on time. It will take a little while to get down the rough road through the trees to the unloading spot."

The boat was on time and soon Rock and Bill were being driven back to the airport in an older 4x4 Suburban. Rock was thinking about getting the planes back to Customs at Fargo before his flight plan expired, but there were other questions on his mind as well.

How long had this scam been going on? Was the Indian village involved and getting paid or were just a few guys doing the labor?

Time would tell, he thought.

It was approaching 21:00 hours as the planes slipped into the Fargo airport for Customs check. It was midnight when the doors were closed on the hangar in Rockford.

So, that's how this is done, said Rock to himself. He was tired and just wanted to crash in a motel before going back home to Montana in the morning.

21

Frank Mullin, Norm Rudy and Rock Smith were again at Bruce Crossing, talking about the Pentoga Compound. Frank said, "Let's ask Boris for some money and tell him we will release him under certain conditions."

Norm said, "If he would put five hundred million in a bank in Switzerland that we could draw on, that would be a start. We could tell him that we would drop him off back in his home area and he could do whatever he wanted with his life – except try to continue with his efforts to rip apart America. He needs to know that if he goes back to his old work that he will get picked up again – never to return to a free life."

"Sounds good to me," said Frank and Rock.

It was another rainy day in Pentoga country with a low cloud cover and strong winds across the lake. Norm had just finished meeting with Boris, who had agreed to the terms of the release. Norm said, "We have less than one million bucks left in our bank. When Boris gets out of here, we need to set the plane down someplace so he can get money transferred to our Swiss bank account before getting him out of the U.S."

Rock was scheduled to show up today, pending flying conditions, so both Frank and Norm were waiting for his call to get his ETA. It had been just over two weeks since Rock had completed his trip to Columbia and been told to expect a second run in the next few weeks. Getting Boris back to his hometown would take three days, depending on the weather.

At 15:00 hours the 206 came in slow and low under the heavy layer of clouds and touched down out front of the compound and taxied up to the swamp grass. Boris was standing under the entry canopy with a blindfold on, looking sharp in a business suit, his hair combed, and without a beard.

With a couple of the Special Forces men on each side of him, he was loaded in the rear seat of the 206 and strapped in. The two Special Forces men went along with Rock to deliver John Boris home.

Rock lifted off the water and flew west for almost an hour at fifteen hundred feet before contacting air space and moving up into radar range. The 206 was headed to the Bemidji Minnesota Airport to allow Boris to call his Swiss bank. Rock was on the phone along with Boris in the discussion to transfer five hundred million in U. S. money from Boris's Swiss account into a Swiss account of RFN, Inc.

The turbo 206 left Bemidji at 18:00 hours, headed for St. Paul, Minnesota, where the leased Cessna Citation was stored. Once Rock was in the air, he filed a flight plan to the Twin Cities and then called the downtown St. Paul Airport, requesting that the Citation jet be pulled from storage and gassed up for a flight at 21:00 hours.

Finally Rock sat back and asked the Special Forces

men to take the blinders off Boris and give him a drink of something and some food. At this point Boris had never seen an outside view of where he had spent the past six months. He had no idea where he was, but hoped he was headed home. Rock filed a flight plan to Rome, Italy, with intermediate stops for gas along the way. He was cleared for takeoff from St. Paul runway 088 at 21:40 hours and was headed east to Bangor, Maine, for his first gas stop.

When the Citation came to a stop at the gas refueling site in Bangor, Rock was met by two Special Forces men that had been set up by Mike Nelson to handle the transfer of Boris to a private home for the night. Everyone needed sleep, some decent food, and lots of quiet time. The drink that Boris had been given on his flight to Bangor put him to sleep.

The plane was met with a stretcher and one of the Special Forces guys was dressed as a medic to assure any onlookers that this flight was one for medical purposes. Rock told the gas operator to fill up all tanks and park the Citation for the night. The group left the airport and headed out into the country north of Bangor. Arriving at the home of one of the Special Forces men, they had a light lunch and went to bed. It was 23:45 hours and the Special Forces men changed off security watch during the night.

The flight to the Mediterranean area was uneventful and at 12:00 hours Boris was settled into a taxi that would take him home. Rock said to John Boris, "John, I hope our agreement with you will last. I do not wish you any ill will and hope the rest of your life is quiet. Just remember that we will find you if you break our agreement, and you will never see sunshine again."

22

Rock had returned home from the Mediterranean nearly three weeks ago and had completed a second delivery of dope from South America. He was now back in his mountain in Montana with his family.

All the freight packages on the planes had received radioactive pins that could be picked up by receivers in the U.S. Mike had set up a surveillance team to track the drugs as they were distributed. Cars, trucks, and small planes were tagged and followed directly to the drop off locations across the mid-west.

No effort was made to pick up the crews doing the work, but time was spent by the Special Forces guys to find as much as possible about the lead contact people. In the near future these guys were going to find themselves in the Pentoga Compound – but not yet.

The second freight drop off went to different locations out east and was followed just as the first distribution had been. It was going to be necessary to continue to pick up the dope for another couple deliveries so the main money could be located.

It was nearly a month before Rock, Norm, and Frank had a plan worked out with Mike to close in on the dope peddlers. There were fifty-two major distribution centers located. Mike was asked to move out his Special Forces teams to pick up the dealers and get them to the compound. The government had not been contacted about the smuggling since many government employees were part of the network.

During the past few weeks, Rock had been flying a large number of the compound crooks away from the compound and letting them off in their hometowns. Each of them was given the same message as was given to Boris – if it were found that they were taking tax payers' funds or creating any legislation that prohibited the U.S. from operating as a free country, they would be picked up and returned to their room in the compound for the rest of their lives. Each one of them had signed a confession and their videos had been made public.

There was a lot of concern about releasing them but short of killing them, this was the plan agreed upon by the Pentoga Compound.

Newspapers, TV and radio programs were on top of the release of dozens of the freed prisoners. Many of the men could not go back to work or go back to their families. Many of them were facing prison or now in prison waiting court results.

With all the missing people and now hundreds of crooks going to jail, very few illegal deals were starting up and fraud on the stock exchange was almost gone. Corporations were hiring thousands of people for producing new products. Unemployment had moved from twenty-two percent eighteen months ago down to less than seven percent around the country. Banks were now servicing the construction companies and lending to the public again. There was almost no money being wasted by the government. Illegal immigration and border drug issues were only minor problems.

23

Norm Rudy was out on his deck in the spring sunshine at Bruce Crossing, Michigan. He still drove the old 2004 Chevy car. There was still half a million in the old pickup stored in the back of the shed. He had been working the past winter driving a snowmobile groomer on the trails to buy food. The difference now was that he smiled a lot, had picked up his old guitar, and was singing some of the country songs of Kenny Rogers.

He was seeing one of his old classmates, Karen Corey from home school years, and this was giving him peace. A few months ago he had stopped at her parent's house and asked what she was doing and where she lived. They told him she was going to school at Houghton Tech and would be graduating this spring from graduate school.

Houghton Tech was up at the far end of Houghton County, just sixty miles north of Bruce Crossing. It took him a couple weeks to get up the nerve to locate her, but finally he had asked her if she would meet him for dinner there in Houghton. He was sitting at a table in the Bear Paw Restaurant when he saw a gorgeous women come in and speak to the front desk clerk. He did not think too much about that, except that she was beautiful.

A minute later a soft voice spoke to him. "Norm, how are you doing?"

He stood up and took her hand. "Karen you look so different from the old days of home school."

Tongue-tied, he finally added, "Come, sit down."

They had lots of catching up to do and each of them talked about the past few years. Norm's sharp green eyes no longer held that blank stare, but were now giving off a warm twinkle; he had put on about thirty pounds and was in perfect condition. They immediately felt excited about each other.

She asked him, "What do you do with your time? Are you working for someone now? Are you still living at the old home place?"

Norm was not too open about his work. He did tell her that he was doing some paperwork for a couple banks out of state. He was able to handle that work from his cabin and enjoyed it.

They began seeing each other once a week for hikes, a movie, or dinner, and though there was no mention of any long range plans with each other, there were some strong hints.

Frank Mullin continued to sell cars in Rockford, Illinois, when he was in town, which wasn't that much. He still lived in his cheap apartment and drove his old truck. His primary job was to stay on top of the Pentoga compound and he would stay up there for a week or so at a time and then drive back home to show people he was still around.

He had been watching March Madness, the college basketball tournament, the past few days and his excitement about sports was returning fast. The spring trout fishing was sucking up a lot of his time and it was good to burn down the logging roads with his ATV and see the spring blossoms and the ducks and geese starting their nests in the wooded ponds.

He was no longer frustrated with life and it now all seemed worthwhile again. America was shaping up and the people would have a future again. He no longer had those dark brooding eyes and there was gentleness showing in his face. He had made contact with a couple of colleges and was planning to start school in the fall.

The Pentoga Compound was filling up again with drug movers and Mike and several other Special Forces guys were now operating the Compound. Rock had hired two more Special Forces pilots to fly floats, so he was able to spend more time with his wife and new baby.

The loss of many of the top drug peddlers had a major impact on the border in Texas and some of the other border states. One of the missing peddlers was named Frank Zanon.

Done with the Talking

New elections were scheduled for November and this time there was no one running that did not understand and commit to total adherence to the U.S. Constitution. It was going to be a great country again.

The Pentoga Compound is still open, well financed, and waiting for those who go astray.

EXCERPT FROM "OUT OF CONTROL"

Rock Smith rolled his cigar in his mouth and squinted his eyes at the last rays of sunlight slipping below the western horizon. He knew he was running out of day. Over the nose of his Cessna 180 he could see Bass Lake and knew he had to get out of the air. It was really getting dark now. He also knew that with the glassy water and the dark shadows he couldn't depend on his depth perception to judge the water surface.

Reaching down along the seat he pulled on thirty degrees of flaps and adjusted his trim. Keeping his eyes on a point of land, the plane settled below the tree tops. He added power to slow the drop and then felt the drag on the floats as they touched the water. He sighed, relaxed his stomach muscles, and eased back on the throttle.

And then all hell broke loose as chunks of glass hit his face like hail and a cool blast of evening air poured through a gaping hole in the windshield. He felt a smashing blow to the side of his head and his hands begin slipping off the yoke. He was falling over against the pilot door and then everything went black.

He could taste the blood flowing across his cheek; he tried to move his hands and legs, but they didn't work. His mind wasn't working clearly, yet he could hear the engine running and feel a heavy vibration in the cockpit. He could smell the gas fumes from the engine and knew something was broken. The old memories of fire in Iraq returned.

Looking out the window, he could see the water shining in the dim moonlight. What happened? Had he crashed? He was beginning to feel a tingling in his feet and hands. He must turn off the engine and master switch to prevent a fire. Reaching out in the dark cockpit, he felt along the dash until his fingers touched the switches. He shut down the engine and all was quiet. A moment passed.

He heard a yell.

"All right, let's finish the job." The sound of the voice was stunning to Rock.

His first reaction was to start the engine and taxi away, but the possibility of fire was too great. He could hear the sound of an outboard motor and knew someone was coming. But more important, someone was trying to kill him. His legs still wouldn't work, yet he had to get free of the plane – and now.

The door handle moved under his hand; the door was ajar. Unfastening his belt, he pulled his numb legs out over the side of the cockpit, looking down at the glistening dark water. Clutching the boat cushion from behind his seat, he dropped it below and slowly slid down the struts into the icy spring water of Bass Lake. He could hear the boat moving down the lake towards the plane.

They were coming for him. The shock of the water seemed to bring some feeling to his legs, yet he knew that his time was short. He leaned across the boat cushion and began to swim towards the dark shoreline.

"He's not in the plane!" someone yelled.

He knew only a moment remained before they found him or before he passed out. He could still feel the warm blood flowing across his neck and down his back. He tried to swim using one hand, holding the other against the wound along his head. He badly needed a bandage to stop the bleeding.

The gravel scraped against his numb feet – he had made it to shore. The cedar trees came down to the water's edge; it was so dark he couldn't see his hands. The scent of cedar and marsh grass and the croaking of frogs came as a pleasant surprise. Carrying the boat cushion, he stumbled through the thick underbrush.

He was exhausted; tears ran down his face from branches hitting across his eyes. The smell of muck hurt his nostrils as he tried to catch his breath. He stepped forward, falling face first into the black night, landing on his knees and then his face. He was sick to his stomach. He couldn't rise.